MESSAGE FOR MURDER

Also by Jerri Kay Lincoln:

Rutledge Historical Society Cozy Mysteries
Message for Murder
Death over Divorce
Kousins Kan't Kill
Rogues to Riches

Memoir
The Dog Who Rescued Me

Children's Books
Cooper's Smile
The Little Unicorn Who Could
Do Bears Poop in the Woods?
Can Pigs Fly?
Why Do Puppy Dogs Have Cold Noses?
The Invisible Lion
La Petite Licorne Qui Pouvait
Das Kleine Einhorn Was Es Kann
The Little Unicorn Who Could Coloring Book
Do Bears Poop in the Woods? Coloring Book

Cookbooks
Ten Delicious Dairy-Free Stevia-Sweetened Ice Cream
Recipes

Message for Murder

Jerri Kay Lincoln

Ralston Store Publishing
P.O. Box 1684
Prescott, Arizona 86302

ISBN 978-1-938322-48-8

Professionally edited by:
Jennifer Hope
www.MesaVerdeMediaServices.com

The reader should note that the nutritional beliefs
and food choices in this book are those of the
characters and not necessarily those of the author or
publisher.

Printed in the USA.

Dedicated to the sleuth in all of us.

CHAPTER ONE

IT LOOKED LIKE a historical society—or most of it did. The historical society was housed in a grand old building—or had been anyway. It was a hulking two-story mostly red brick building, with two broad windows on the bottom floor, and three much smaller windows outlined in white on the top floor, with a zigzag pattern of dark gray bricks above the top windows. She was a beauty. One window on the second floor looked cracked. Hanging from the top of the building was a large wooden sign that read Rutledge Historical Society.

The only element of the illustrious old building that looked out of place was the coffee shop next door. It wasn't really next door because it was part of the building. The front of the coffee shop portion of the building had been painted bright yellow, with big letters across the front window that said Rutledge Koffee Korner Kafe. The "R" in Rutledge was stylized so it looked more like a K. So it appeared to say Kutledge Koffee Korner Kafe. How the city fathers approved that, I'll never know. If it had been the city mothers that never would have happened.

1

It wasn't like that when I lived here—although that was many years ago. And I hadn't been back once in all that time except a few days ago for the job interview.

Rutledge, Arizona, was located southwest of Flagstaff and northwest of Sedona. The road from Sedona to Rutledge was dirt, windy with drop-offs on either side, and mostly reserved for those brave souls who owned four-wheel drive vehicles. To get here from Flagstaff, you took the interstate to a two-lane highway south to Coyote Moon and then east to Rutledge. That's the way most people came—most of the sane people, anyway.

Taking a deep breath, I walked across the street toward the building. Clouds hung over the mountains obscuring all but the tops of them. The rest of the sky was that brilliant shade of blue that made you feel like you could take a bite right out of it. The low-hanging clouds were the last remnants of yesterday's unseasonable rain.

Directly across the street from the historical society was Johansen's Hardware Store. It was on the corner of High Street and End Street, which had been aptly named a hundred years ago. The only place End Street led to was River Road—a pleasantly named place that was run-down and falling apart. The only reason the town of Rutledge hadn't insisted it be removed from existence altogether was because there was only one way to get there, End Street, and the only people who found themselves on River Road were those who wanted to be there. It used to be the old dumping grounds before people realized that the Rutledge River was not meant to be a dump. Now it was car parts stores and junk yards filled with old cars.

I had parked on End Street next to the hardware

store, because it was the only place around that didn't have parking meters. At least that hadn't changed. There was no way I'd park in the hardware store's parking lot. Old man Johansen used to go out to the parking lot himself to check the cars. If their owners weren't in there shopping, he'd have the cars towed away. Did he even still own the store? He was old back then, and that was many years ago.

Before putting my hand on the doorknob, I looked up. Rutledge Historical Society. With that bright yellow side of the building, it made it look more like the Rutledge Hysterical Society! Although the sign on the door said *Closed*, I turned the knob, the door opened, and I walked inside. Since it was nine o'clock, I turned the sign to *Open*.

"Hello! Anybody home? Hello!" I was about to step into the back and see if anyone was there when the phone rang. Since no one else was picking it up from another room, I grabbed it. "Rutledge Historical Society! . . . Yes, we are open today. We close at five o'clock. . . . You're welcome. Goodbye."

After hanging up the phone, I set my coffee on the desk, slipped off my blue cardigan sweater, and sank into the soft desk chair. If someone was in the back, I decided, they would have heard me. I closed my eyes and took a sip of the coffee that I had gotten from Dunkin' Donuts. It was still hot, thankfully. Had I gotten it next door at the coffee shop, I might have run into my cousin, Cruella DeVille.

That wasn't her real name, of course. Her real name was Kasey Brannigan, but I've been calling her Cruella DeVille since first grade when she stole my first boyfriend, Conrad Hayes. Although in all honesty, she

3

didn't steal him and he wasn't my boyfriend. My first crush would be more accurate. Still, I wanted him and she got him. That was as bad as stealing the Dalmatians, wasn't it?

Cruella DeVille did get me this job though. I should feel grateful for that, shouldn't I? I guess I was. After that slob left me, I ended up in that crummy motel with no money and no job. But that's a whole "'nother" story, isn't it? Although, I could argue that technically *I* left him.

This job came vacant unexpectedly when the elderly woman who ran the place fell down the stairs and died. Betty Wellesley was a friendly woman whom everyone liked, so from what I understand, it was really sad. They needed someone to fill her spot straightaway, and since I was available and cousin Cruella vouched for me, I got the job after a brief interview.

Shaking my head and frowning, I took a deep breath and then another sip of the coffee. It hit the spot. Okay, now that I had my brains back, I looked around the room. To my left was a glassed-in gift shop that extended farther down the hallway. Its entrance/exit was by the other office that was through the hallway and behind me. I sat at a big desk by the big front window with a clear view of Johansen's Hardware Store. It was still called that, so he must still own it.

To my right sat another small desk with a large computer monitor on it. The keyboard was below in a small drawer made for that purpose. The tower sat on the floor on the left-hand side underneath the desk. The swivel chair that I sat on was in the perfect position to swivel over and work on the computer. That is, if I didn't hit my knee on the wooden desk in the process. If you hear me scream, you'll know I whacked my poor knee.

Directly across from the computer desk on the opposite wall was a tall filing cabinet, and beside that, behind me, was a large fish tank. That will be infinitely annoying, I mused. They make noise all the time and they stink. I hated fish tanks. Above the fish tank was a beautiful picture of the Rutledge Historical Society building before the Rutledge Koffee Korner Kafe had taken possession of part of it and painted it that hideous yellow. Maybe someday the building could be restored to its former glory.

The desk in front of me was one of those old-fashioned huge wooden affairs with six roomy drawers. The bottom drawer on each side was large enough for files to fit into. I opened the bottom right drawer, and sure enough, there were several file folders in there, labeled Last Year, This Year, Permissions, and a dozen others. When I opened the bottom left drawer, it was empty, so I stuck my purse inside. Okay then. The woman who worked here before me, poor soul, was left-handed.

The front door opened, the bell attached to the top of it jingling. I stood up when I saw it was Martha Goldstein, the woman who had hired me. She came through the door with a broad smile on her face. Martha was in her sixties, with gray hair and smiling gray eyes. She was dressed in a stylish print dress with matching shoes that gave her an appearance of youth that belied her years, and I liked her. Martha reached out and clasped my hand in both of hers. They were warm.

"So good to see you, Lorry! Right on time, too." She looked past my shoulder. "Is Petra in the back?"

"No, no one is here."

"Really? Petra—her name is actually Priscilla, but she prefers Petra—is always on time. I wonder where she is." After tilting her head and pondering for a moment, she looked at me. "Ah, well. You're here now. Most people when visiting prefer to look on their own. Petra can give you the documentation"—she glanced toward the desk —"or maybe it's in there. Well, would you like me to take you through again?" She took a step toward the back when her cell phone rang.

"Hello? . . . Yes, I'll be right back! Bye!" Stepping backward, she opened the door. "Sorry. Gotta run. I'll see you later. Petra should be here any moment now. I can't think where she might be." And Martha was out the door in a flash.

Sitting back down at the desk, I drank the rest of my coffee and threw the empty cup in the garbage. My eyes itched, my nose started running, and then I sneezed. I wasn't getting a cold, so what was that about? Looking around, I determined there was nothing nearby that I could be allergic to, so I shrugged and looked through the files in the right-hand drawer. There it was, Exhibits, squeezed between Tropical Fish and Books I've Read. When I pulled it out and set it on the desk in front of me, I realized that it was time for a bathroom break. The coffee had gone right through me.

As I looked through the glass windows of the gift store, I passed another desk on my left. That must be Priscilla's desk. What was that other name that Martha used? It was something weird, I knew that much. There was a slight turn to the right, but as I was about to walk through the passageway, I felt another sneeze coming on. My head lifted automatically—I think it's mandatory that heads do that when you sneeze—and as I sneezed my eyes closed, also automatically, and I stepped forward. My foot ran into something, and I had to grab the doorjamb to catch myself from falling.

When my sneeze concluded, I opened my eyes and quickly covered my mouth with my hand to stifle my scream. My foot had hit a dead body.

CHAPTER TWO

WITH MY HAND still over my mouth, my mind raced. I know it sounds stupid, but the first thing that came to my mind was, wouldn't they have taken away the dead body by now? It had been days since she died. The reason I thought that—see, it's not as stupid as it sounds—was because I had been told Betty Wellesley had been found at the foot of the stairs, having tumbled down them carrying a box of books. But this woman, who looked the same age as the first deceased, was also *resting* at the foot of the stairs. There were no books around. So who was this?

I stumbled back to my desk, one hand on my mouth and the other on my heart. I sat down and began to search frantically for Martha's number at the City of Rutledge—as if Rutledge was actually a city, but no need to quibble about that at the moment. After a minute of fruitless searching, I decided to just dial 9-1-1. So after I sneezed again, that's what I did.

"Hello! I'd like to report a—a—a dead body! Yeah, that's it! A dead body! That's what I'd like to do is report a dead body!" I didn't give the dispatcher time to say anything. Words kept spewing out of my mouth as if I had no control over them. Because I didn't. "I'm at the Hysterical—I mean Historical Society!" Breathless, I finally stopped talking. "No! I didn't kill her! I just found her! . . . Yes, I'm sure she's dead. She's just laying there and not moving! What would you call it?" Okay, I was getting a little flustered, but wouldn't you be if someone asked you such stupid questions? At least they seemed stupid at the time. "Fine. I'll be here."

Desperate as I was for something familiar—finding a dead body is not the most common thing to happen to a person—I stuck my hand into the garbage can and pulled out my empty coffee cup. I held it up to my mouth and willed it to have a drop or two left in it. All that I got was a fragment of lint. At least I hoped it was lint. I spit it out as the door burst open—the bell almost jingling off its tether—and the sheriff strode on through without saying a word. Maybe he didn't see me. I'm not exactly petite—okay, I'm a little on the chunky side—but I blend in rather well.

A minute later, two deputies rushed in, looking twelve years old and smelling like a perfume factory. They looked at me questioningly, and I pointed toward the back. "He went that-a-way!" Without a word of acknowledgement, they tromped into the back room. Don't parents teach their kids to say "please" and "thank-you" anymore? What's becoming of the world today?

I opened each drawer of the desk hoping for a telephone book. It's amazing how many places don't have phone books anymore and rely on the internet for their information. But I didn't want to turn on the computer in case there was something special about it that I might mess up. Finding nothing, I stood up and took the few steps to the gray filing cabinet. I searched through all those drawers—no phone book anywhere. Sitting back down at the big wooden desk, I moved the file folder to the side, looked at the blotter, and realized that it had phone numbers scrawled all over it. Many of the numbers had no names attached, some of them were crossed out, and out of all the numbers and notes on there, one of them was in a different hand.

As I pondered the meaning of that, I looked out the window to watch a bright red ambulance double park and then put the red flashers on. Two men darted out, opened the back, and pulled out a gurney. Horrified, I got to my feet to open the door for them. As they streaked past me, I panicked. "Oh, good heavens. She's not still alive, is she?"

One of the fifteen-year-olds carrying the gurney—they both looked a few years older than the twelve-year-old deputies—said, "No, ma'am. She's not." At least they didn't reek of perfume.

I staggered backward and fell into the desk chair, which swiveled around and rolled toward the fish tank. I barely managed to stop myself in time. Killing the fish. Now that would be a tragedy. Rolling back to the desk, I ran my hand along the blotter until I found the number written in a different hand and punched the numbers on the phone.

It was the right number, as I had expected. "Martha Goldstein, please. . . . Okay, thank you. . . . Martha? Something terrible has happened." After I briefly described to her the events of the morning, she said she would come over as soon as she could. We hung up.

"I could kill for a cup of coffee," I muttered to myself

as the ambulance boys traipsed by with a body bag on the gurney.

"Pardon me, ma'am?" one of the boys asked.

"Oh, nothing! Sorry! Nothing!" Talking about killing when there was a dead body going by was probably not the smartest thing to come out of my mouth. And that's when it hit me. The chances of that woman *also* falling down the stairs were probably minimal. Which meant, oh, dear, that someone had probably murdered her.

As that thought went through my head, the two young deputies paraded past me whispering to themselves. A few minutes later, the sheriff came out and walked right up to me. Apparently I didn't blend in all *that* well.

He put out his hand. "My name is Billy Madrigal, ma'am. I'd like to ask you a few questions."

CHAPTER THREE

SHERIFF BILLY HAD a strong grip, a tight build, black hair peeking out from beneath his hat, and dazzling blue eyes. In short, he was a hunk. Too bad he was a cop though. I hated cops with their arrogance, better-than-thou attitude, and power-hungry ways. Besides, what kind of name was Billy for a sheriff? It reminded me of Sheriff John, or Mr. Greenjeans or Big Bird, or something—anything but law enforcement.

"My name is Lorry. Lorry Lockharte," I stammered.

He stood above me looking down. He was tall. Dark and handsome, too. It was disarming. The whole thing made me feel guilty. I was about to confess to everything when I thought it might be wiser just to stand up. So I did.

"Hello, Lorry," he said. "Were you the first one in today?"

"I—I don't know. The door was open when I got here, but nobody was here—well, except for—" I nodded my head to the side toward where the body had lain. "You know."

"Yes, ma'am."

Before he could say anything else, I blurted out, "But I didn't do it, I swear."

A quick smile crossed his lips and disappeared before I had a chance to get a good look at it. "Yes, I know. She was killed sometime last night would be my guess, but the medical examiner will have to verify that." He looked around the room, and his eyes settled on the front door. "What have you touched since you came in?"

"I touched the outside door handle, of course, and—"

"Did you touch the one on the inside?"

"Oh, dear. Not until the ambulance boys arrived. I opened the door for them." I winced. "Sorry."

"That's all right, ma'am. You will need to come down to the sheriff's station and have your fingerprints taken, though, so we can rule you out."

"You won't arrest me for past parking ticket violations, will you?"

"Why, do you have any?"

"Not that I know of, but I thought I'd ask." I smiled at him. He was awfully cute. Definitely too bad he was a cop.

He smiled back. A bright shining smile that could almost make you *forget* he was a cop. "Don't worry then, I'll try to overlook them."

I was about to reply with another witty remark when Martha came through the door. "Hello, Billy. You've met Lorry, then?"

"Yes, I've met her." He turned his head to glance at me and he winked! "I'll need her to come down to the station so we can take her fingerprints. And if she has no parking violations, I'll let her go." He chuckled.

Martha looked at him and then at me and realized it was a joke. It *was* a joke, wasn't it?

"Come outside with me for a minute, will you, Martha?" Sheriff Billy looked at me. "Nice meeting you, Miss Lockharte. I'll see you at the station." He tipped his Smokey the Bear hat at me. Oh, pardon me. Sometime in the early 1990s Smokey somehow lost his middle name. So Sheriff Billy tipped his Smokey Bear hat at me.

The two of them walked outside, talked for a few minutes, and then Billy drove away and Martha walked back inside, turning the *Open* sign to *Closed*. So much for my first day of work.

"Lorry, Billy wants us to close for the day, so forensics can come in here and do a complete work-up. It appears that Gwen was murdered." She sniffled, but I didn't realize why at the time.

I shivered. "Who was she?"

"That's the curious part, isn't it? She's Betty's sister."

"Betty? Is she the one who fell down the stairs the other day?"

"Yes, she is. Anyway, they'll be here most of the morning, so, if you don't mind, I'd like you to stay— make sure no one else comes in and gets in their way."

"No problem. I'm happy to stay."

"Great. Has Petra been in?"

"No, she hasn't." And that's when it hit me. Petra Priscilla must have done it! That's why she wasn't there when I arrived. She did the deed and then escaped across the border! Or wherever it is that murderers go after they do the dirty.

"That's also curious. She's never late." Martha pursed her lips, shook her head, and then nodded. "Well, I'm sure there is a good explanation. She's quite reliable.

"So, anyway, stay the rest of the day, and although nobody except forensics will be here, you can study the documentation on the exhibits and familiarize yourself with them. When Petra arrives, probably later this afternoon, she can give you the full tour.

"I need to get back right now. You can get fingerprinted tomorrow sometime when Petra is here. All set now? Goodbye, Lorry. Sorry for such a ruckus on your first day here." As she went out the door, I heard her mumble, "Poor Gwen. Poor Betty." And I saw her wipe her nose as she walked by the window.

They were friends! They must have been. Probably both Betty and her sister. Rutledge was still a small town —certainly Martha was close to both of them. So this wasn't just a murder, it was a personal murder. And I was certain that Petra Priscilla did it.

As I was thinking about that, the door—which still had the *Closed* sign on it—flew open and a blur of purple and pink went by.

"Excuse me," I called. "We're closed. Sorry for the inconvenience." I stood up to follow the blur and kick it out.

From the back, she shouted, "I work here."

I walked over to the room behind mine. "You must be Priscilla, then."

"Petra! My name is Petra. And you must be Lorry."

Priscilla or Petra was not wearing pink and purple. That was her hair color. Each ear had multiple earrings starting at the top and working their way down, and the bottom ones were big loops that nearly reached her shoulders. She had piercings on her eyebrow and the side of her nose, and when she spoke to me I saw that she had a stud on her tongue, as well. The tattoo on her hand was of a small blue flower. She wore a skimpy blouse exposing her midriff to show another piercing on

15

her bellybutton. Her capris were black with big red polka dots. Where do kids come up with clothes these days? The sandals on her feet had a decorative strap around her ankle.

"Yes, I'm Lorry. Did you come in earlier this morning?"

Priscilla had been rummaging through her desk, but she looked up sharply at the question. "No, why?"

"Because a woman—Gwen—seemed to have been murdered here. Do you know anything about that?"

"No! Why would I?" Standing up, she said, "Gwen? Really? Are you sure?" Then without waiting for an answer, she grabbed her purse from the bottom drawer. "Look, I'd love to chat with you all day, but I need to get back to school. I'll see you later."

Oh, great, I thought. The pink and purple kaleidoscope raced past me and out the door. And then my eyes watered and I sneezed again.

CHAPTER FOUR

BEFORE ANYTHING ELSE occurred—especially finding any more dead bodies—I had to visit the restroom. My need had become urgent, and my aborted trip back there when I found the body seemed like hours ago. Walking to the back, I came to the spot where I had found poor Gwen. There was an outline on the floor, just like in the movies. I turned left and opened the bathroom door. It was a small room, but clean. Opposite the toilet was a service cabinet made of wood and painted beige. Besides the pink paisley wall paper, it looked like an industrial bathroom, replete with split toilet seat. Why? Does it honestly save money not to have the seat go all the way around the outside? That was one thing that I hated. On the floor was a small bowl of water. What was that for? After finishing my business and washing and drying my hands, I returned to my desk.

I was dying for a cup of coffee, but I didn't want to risk seeing my cousin Kasey—formerly known as Cruella DeVille—next door, so I sat there and suffered. Although I knew intellectually that coffee was a stimulant, I wanted the coffee to relax me. Sometimes, when you're stressed, something familiar can be relaxing. Coffee was familiar. Then I realized my last thought about dying for a cup of coffee. Dying for a cup of coffee or killing for a cup of coffee were probably the wrong things to think about since in the last week two people had died—or maybe been killed—in the very building that I sat in.

Sighing, I picked up the Exhibits folder. Before I had a chance to even open it, the two twelve-year-old deputies appeared at the door without entering. As they knelt down, one of them opened his kit and dusted the outside door handle for fingerprints. When they finished, they opened the door, nodded acknowledgement, and dusted the inside door handle. Then they stood up and walked toward the back. Before they disappeared, though, one of them turned around and saluted me. I did the only thing I could think of: I saluted back. Had I been standing up, I would have clicked my heels as well—since I *was* wearing heels—but alas, I was comfortably seated, so I stayed there.

Since the black dust was on the inside and outside handles, I searched in my purse until I found the tissues, and then I cleaned both handles, tossed the tissues in the trash, and sat back down again. I opened the file on the exhibits and began reading. Strangely enough, although called Exhibits, it had a lot of general history on Rutledge that was interesting. Some of it I knew, some I didn't.

For instance, I knew Rutledge had originally been separated by the river into East Rutledge and West Rutledge. And when the casino was built in the 1980s, since it was called Coyote Moon Casino, the City of West Rutledge renamed itself Coyote Moon, Arizona. And when that happened, East Rutledge changed its

18

name to Rutledge. If there was no West Rutledge, then East Rutledge didn't make sense any longer.

Rutledge, with only the one narrow bridge separating it from Coyote Moon, became the small, perhaps obsolete city, while Coyote Moon grew and grew with the casino and its jobs paving the way. It started out just hiring Native Americans, but soon there weren't enough in the area to meet all the work requirements.

The more people that moved there, the bigger the town became. More to the point, Rutledge was the town, and Coyote Moon was the city. There, one would find—besides the casino—the local college, the huge movie theaters with multiple showings of multiple films, large chain grocery-stores, and of course all the big box stores. Coyote Moon had the conveniences of a large city while Rutledge remained firmly ensconced in the small-town past of Arizona. And truthfully, most residents liked it that way. The ones who didn't, moved to Coyote Moon.

Personally, I thought I loved Rutledge until I started college in Coyote Moon. Still, I came home to the peace and quiet of Rutledge as often as I could. Until I met Eddie. His nickname was Fast Eddie, which should have been a clue if I hadn't been so pigheaded and blind to all the red flags waved in front of me.

He was trouble from the start—he got kicked out of school for cheating after we had been dating for only a week. Was that enough to dissuade me from a disastrous future? Of course not. Job after job he got fired from for various nefarious reasons—mostly involving money—which he then took to the casino and either lost every cent he had or else came home with overflowing pockets of money and handfuls of roses.

And did I mention the other women in his life? One

woman was not enough for Fast Eddie. When he was winning, one woman couldn't contain him. When he was losing, one woman wasn't enough to comfort him. So what would you do with such a rapscallion of a man as this? Well, what I did was marry him.

By the time I concluded that bitter reminiscence, the forensic boys had finished. They walked through and the same one who saluted me before, did it again. I saluted back and then returned to the folder. There were twenty-five individual exhibit sheets in the folder, some of them short, some of them quite lengthy. And not all of them were marked *current*. By the time I finished reading the last one, it was late afternoon.

The phone hadn't rung the rest of the day after that first phone call, and no one ever showed up. Although with the *Closed* sign on the front, they may have come while I was absorbed in the Exhibit file, and I might not have noticed. It had been a long day, half exciting and half boring, so I yawned.

At that moment, the front door opened and the pink and purple kaleidoscope strolled in. "Hello, Lorry," she said without turning her head and without stopping.

"Hello, Priscilla," I said.

"It's Petra! Everyone calls me Petra!" She stood there with her hands on her hips staring at me. "Priscilla is from the Roman meaning venerable, classical. The Puritans often used that name. Petra is from the Greek meaning stone, rock. Which do you think suits me better?"

Not bothering to answer, I ignored her and went back to feeling bored. Stone does suit her better—she's probably a stoner pothead. After a few minutes of hearing her shuffling items around and making a quiet

20

cell phone call in a hushed voice, she yelled from her office, "So how do you like it so far?"

Standing up, I stretched, sneezed, and then walked into her office, leaning on the wall that separated us. Her office was smaller than mine, but more modern. Her desk was a standard computer desk with the keyboard in the middle drawer. The computer itself was one of those Apple all-in-one contraptions with a big monitor. There was a chair in front of the desk with its back against the side wall, because the space was too small for it to face the desk.

"You mean if I don't count running into a dead body in my first hour here? Fine. Except the fish tank. I can't stand fish tanks. They stink and make noise."

"Fish tanks don't stink! And the *sound* it makes is called 'white noise.' It's supposed to be soothing."

"Ah, whatever!" I tossed my head and acted like it didn't matter anyway. Because it didn't. "Say, can you give me a tour of the exhibits today?"

She flicked on her computer and shook her head. "Sorry. Since I wasn't here this morning, I'm a little behind."

"Yeah," I narrowed my eyes wondering if I could somehow wangle a confession out of her. "Where *were* you this morning?"

She put both hands on the top of her desk, turned her head to look at me, and narrowed her eyes right back. "That is *none* of your business." Then she faced her computer, and without looking at me, she said, "By the way, you are welcome to turn on your computer. You won't hurt anything." She looked at me. "I know *older* people are afraid of computers, so you don't have to worry."

21

"*Older?* What do you mean *older?* I'm barely older than you are!" That wasn't exactly true. I was probably twice her age, but she meant it as an insult, so I had to act the part. As I was about to make a more witty repartee, I heard the jingling sound of the front door opening. It was my cousin Kasey.

CHAPTER FIVE

MY COUSIN KASEY wore a bright yellow waitress uniform that matched the front of the building, with *Rutledge Koffee Korner Kafe* stitched on one pocket and *Kasey* stitched on the other. She had white, sensible waitress-type shoes. That's one reason I could never be a waitress: I couldn't bear for anyone to see me in shoes like that. My motto was, if they weren't heels, then they weren't worth wearing.

"Lorry. So good to see you," Kasey said as she hugged me.

"You, too, Kasey. Thanks so much for getting me this job. I needed it! And I appreciate it!"

She swished her hand brushing away my thanks. "Oh, it's nothing. Glad I could help. And Martha needed someone in here right away. You were the first one to come to mind. Especially since there was a fish tank in here." Nodding to the fish tank, she continued. "I know how much you love fish tanks!"

Before I had a chance to even grunt, Petra called out from the other room. "I thought you hated fish tanks because they stink and make noise?"

"No, Petra, it was Eddie who hated fish tanks. Lorry always loved them."

"Yeah, I guess it *was* Eddie who hated them," I admitted. "Maybe I just caught it."

Kasey sat on the edge of my desk. "So I heard what happened today. What a first day, you've had, huh? Sorry I couldn't come in earlier. Lily was sick, and I couldn't find anyone to sit with her until my neighbor came home a couple of hours ago."

Kasey hardly took a breath between sentences. Married to her high school sweetheart, John, they had two children: Lily, who was six, and an infant named after a Weather Channel storm, Zandor. Thank goodness she didn't name him Goliath. Can you imagine the locker room teasing when the kid reached high school?

"So, anyway," Kasey continued, "what happened this time? Why'd Eddie leave?"

I shook my head slowly from side to side and pouted. "Kasey, you make it sound like this has happened a dozen times before. Oh, wait. It has."

She laughed. "Come on. Tell me. One thing about Eddie, he was always entertaining."

"Well, you know we went to the Grand Canyon," I started. "We went on one of those mule rides down to the bottom. And on the way back up—we were almost to the top—Eddie yells out, 'You know, Lorry, your butt is bigger than that mule's, and frankly, I'm tired of following it. As soon as we get home, I'm leaving!'" I looked at Kasey. "Aren't you going to laugh?"

Kasey smiled. "Well, it *is* kind of funny."

"Yeah, it's funny!" said Petra from the other room.

"Yeah, it was funny all right. It was so funny that as

soon as we climbed off the mules at the top, Eddie went to the restroom, and I drove the car home and left him there with no transportation!"

"You didn't!" said Kasey.

I shrugged. "Yes, I did. He deserved it. But Eddie still came out ahead. I found out two things when I got home. One, there was a three-day eviction notice on the door of the house, because the bank had foreclosed on our loan. And two, Eddie had cleaned out our joint bank account. And on top of that, there was a phone message on our landline from old Joe MacDonald's daughter. He had a stroke and so his business was officially closed. And I was officially out of a job. But you already knew that part."

Kasey nodded and continued like she didn't even hear me, and she probably didn't. Listening wasn't her forte. Talking was. "Oh, man! Rough! Did the daughter give you any severance pay?"

"She wasn't going to until I marched over to her house, showed her the three-day eviction notice and told her that I would park my fat butt on her doorstop if she didn't come up with some money for me. I worked for Joe for over ten years! You can't do that to a loyal employee!"

"What happened with the house? Why didn't you know they were going to foreclose?"

"Because I thought that idiot scammer Eddie had been paying the mortgage. Every time I gave him the money the previous five months, he told me he had paid it. And when the notices came, he got the mail before I did and threw them away! I found out about that after the fact. *Way* after the fact." I shook my head and frowned.

"So where are you staying now?"

"The old West Rutledge Motel at the edge of town." It was an old motel that refused to change its name after the rest of the businesses in the city changed theirs to Coyote Moon.

"That place is a dung heap!" called Petra from the other room. "You're going to get bedbugs or something from there! You need to leave there right away! You might bring them here!"

"She's right, Lorry. That place is awful. You can't stay there."

"Well, smarty pantses, where do you suggest I go? It's the only place I can afford right now."

"Martha has a bed and breakfast here in Rutledge. It's not far, and I'm sure she'd give you a great deal," said Petra.

"That's a good idea," agreed Kasey.

"You both are forgetting something important here. I have *no* money!"

"Martha will give you an advance," said Petra. "Just ask her. And if she doesn't, I can loan you some money."

That hushed me. That little kaleidoscope queen, who couldn't have been more than sixteen years old, offered to loan *me* money. Involuntarily, I put my hand on my heart because it touched me so.

Kasey looked at her watch. "Oh, I have to run. I was due back a couple of minutes ago. See ya later!"

"Bye, Kasey," I said as she buzzed out the door. I exhaled slowly and walked into the back room to talk to Petra. What I saw when I got there chilled me to the core. There on her desk, was a fat black cat, and Petra was stroking it. I took one unbelieving look, my head went up, my eyes closed, and I sneezed.

CHAPTER SIX

"WHAT IS THAT *thing* on your desk?" I choked out between sniffles. Then I rubbed my itchy eyes and sneezed again.

"What? You've never seen a cat before? This is Rocky. Betty rescued him from a raccoon fight, and he has lived here ever since."

"That's why I've been sneezing!"

"You're allergic to cats? Too bad. Rocky isn't going anywhere." She said it matter-of-factly and continued petting him.

It didn't take a genius to realize that she was implying that *I* was the one who had to go. Even an idiot could figure that one out. Oh, wait. Forget that. I looked at my watch. Five o'clock on the nose. "I guess it's time for me to go home. Goodbye." As I stomped out, I sneezed again.

Walking across the street still sneezing, I almost tripped over the curb just at the moment when my eyes closed. After unlocking my car, I stepped into it, drove to the bridge, crossed it, stopped at a convenience store for a cheap TV dinner, and then pulled into the motel

27

parking lot.

It was a horrible place. Not only was the paint peeling all over, but here and there great chunks of plaster had fallen off. The door to my room, number eight, had a bullet hole through the middle of it, patched with something that looked like toothpaste. It was still sticky. Don't ask me how I know that. The number eight had lost one of the three nails that held it on—the top one—and the bottom one was about to go, so the number hung askew, looking like an infinity sign instead of an eight.

When I walked in, the smell of stale urine assaulted me. When I spent most days inside the room, I had become used to the urine smell, but whenever I entered for the first time in several hours, the smell greeted me like an unwanted visitor. Surprise! Guess who's here! I closed the door and immediately opened all the windows. Make that window. There was only one. It was a dark and dingy room. It was the kind of place people came to commit suicide. I had come here because it was all I could afford. But now I finally had a job, so I hoped that I could get something more livable soon.

I popped the TV dinner into the food-encrusted microwave and changed clothes. After I put my slacks on, the microwave clicked off. It was the second microwave since I moved into the room. The first one's light came on, but nothing happened. The light was on, but nobody was home. So the motel exchanged it. But the current one didn't work much better. It kept turning itself off before the time was finished. I started it again and finished getting dressed. I didn't have to worry about anyone walking by while I got dressed in front of the window, because I was the only idiot stupid enough or broke enough to stay here.

I sat in front of the television eating my dinner. Rabbit ears adorned the top of the sixteen-inch television, and I could barely make out the voices over the static. Luckily, the best channel was ABC, so I could still watch *Gray's Anatomy* and hear most of the conversations.

There was no phone in the room, but I had my cell. The room did have a lock on the door, and the towels in the bathroom, although every one had suspicious looking stains, all smelled freshly laundered. The shower stall was dark with mold growing in the corners. Thinking about Petra mentioning bedbugs, I pulled up the sheets on the bed. No telltale signs of bedbugs, thank heaven.

I put the empty TV dinner tray in the trashcan outside my room and then slumped down on the bed. It could be worse. I could be on the street and sleeping in the gutter with no roof over my head. You know what they say, a tarnished roof is better than no roof at all. I fell asleep wallowing in my own misery.

The next morning I dragged myself out of bed and into the bathroom. While I was brushing my teeth, a cockroach crawled across the sink. I gagged on the toothpaste and almost barfed. Okay, I decided. That was it. The motel was a horrible place, and I couldn't stand it a moment longer. Second thing to do this morning was to go to Martha and ask for an advance. First thing was to go get fingerprinted.

Dunkin' Donuts, my breakfast place of choice, always had good hot coffee and fresh donuts. Today was a chocolate jelly roll day. They're the best. I finished the donut as I crossed the bridge and wiped my hands on one of those wet tidy towels that I had bought for the purpose.

Before driving to the sheriff's station, I drove by the historical society to make sure the kaleidoscope girl had showed up today. The sign said *Open* so I turned around and drove back the other way. The sheriff's station was on Main Street in the same place where it'd been for years.

Not that many years. When I was a kid, the old wooden sheriff's station burned down and badly injured a prisoner. That's when they built the new one. A bright white concrete building with green trim and replete with a raised flower bed encircling the bottom. What was in the flower bed—not flowers, but local small plants—could use a little more care. Besides the plants, though, the place was all spiffy and looked more like a large house than a sheriff's station. Behind the station and attached on either side, was a high chain-link fence topped with barbed wire.

The strange thing was that said sheriff's station, which was in a pleasant area of town, had bars on all the windows, as if they were trying to keep someone from stealing the furniture. There were no prisoners in there; I knew that. When the building was rebuilt, the jail part of it was not included. All prisoners go to the jail in Coyote Moon. There was a holding cell that was only used for brief periods of time—hours rather than days.

I parked in the lot next to a dirty pickup truck with half a ripped-off bumper sticker that said "other car" and on the bottom "a horse." The truck had a load of hay in the back. On the other side of me was the single handicapped space.

It was good that I wasn't a ninety-eight-pound weakling, because the solid, heavy door required a certain amount of oomph to enter. The place was built like a fortress. When I walked inside, a buzzer went off announcing a person of importance. Me! In front of me, there was a door leading to the back, a door with a combination lock attachment was to the left of me, and to the right was a glassed-in reception area. The woman who greeted me wore a turquoise blue—my favorite color—polo shirt with "Civilian Officer" stitched over the pocket. She smiled at me and asked how she could help.

I smiled back. She was friendly and had a kind face. So what was she doing in a sheriff's station? "I'm here to have my fingerprints taken." When she raised her eyebrows, I added, "I'm not a suspect or anything. I just —"

Sheriff Billy came walking out from the back room, and as he walked past me he said, "*Every*body is a suspect!" He winked at me but didn't smile. Then he walked out the front door. I'd accuse him of going to the donut store, but it wouldn't be much of an insult since I had just come from there.

CHAPTER SEVEN

"DON'T WORRY ABOUT him," the turquoise-shirted woman said. "He's always joking."

"I hope so. I was afraid he was aiming to throw me in jail." I don't know why I said that, but it seemed clever at the time.

"I'll be right with you," she said.

Half a minute later she emerged from the side door that had the combination lock on the outside. "In here. It won't take long."

She led me into a small white room with industrial-strength carpeting. There was a counter on one side of the room and a desk with two chairs on the other that was facing a barred window. In the corner sat a tall artificial plant that needed dusting. Or watering. Whatever it is you do to artificial plants. They've never been my style.

There was a sign above the counter that said, "Why Fingerprints are Rejected." So what if they are rejected? Do you need to get new fingers if that happens?

"Will you be more comfortable sitting or standing?"

I shrugged. "Doesn't matter to me."

She pulled on black surgical gloves and said, "Okay, give me your hand."

"Should I remove it first?" I asked.

She chuckled and took my outstretched hand. Starting with my thumb, she made a rolling motion over the ink pad and then over the card she was putting the prints on. When she finished the right hand, she did the left hand. "All finished!" She looked at the card to make sure there were no smudges. "Looks good!"

"Do they make me look innocent?" I asked. She looked at me and shook her head with a smile. "Where can I wash my hands?"

"Oh! Here, use this." She pointed to a large container of hand cleaner. "We don't have a public restroom, sorry."

I put the cleaner on my hands and rubbed it off with the paper towels left beside the container. I had to do it two times, and even after that, the fingers still had traces of the ink. "Thanks for your help!"

"Thank you for coming in!"

We said our goodbyes, and I struggled with the heavy door and walked to the parking lot. After stepping into the car and taking a sip of the still warm coffee, I drove to the Town Offices.

The parking lot was behind the modern pink and gray concrete building. The walkway leading from the lot to the building had a sign that said "Town Administration Offices." Then it listed several different offices housed within, including the Town Clerk. That was Martha's office. That had been her job since before I left Rutledge, but I had never met her back then.

I followed the path that passed a flagpole with the American flag and the Arizona flag. At the base of it was a large ornamental rock with a sign that had the Rutledge seal on it, which showed a javelina. It was a baby javelina with a slight smile on its face, because most people were either scared of them or just plain didn't like them. I guess those people couldn't see their inner beauty.

The door to the building had Rutledge Town Offices in prominent gold lettering. Just inside was what appeared to be a small waiting area, including a bulletin board with town business flyers plastered all over it, chairs, and a tall magazine rack filled from top to bottom with an assortment of magazines. Everything from *Sports Illustrated* to *People Magazine* to *Highlights for Children*. Although I almost got sidetracked by the story about the most recent flamboyant Hollywood divorce, I finally opened the glass doors and walked into the main part of the building. The interior was all glass and wood, with a vinyl wood floor. Is that stuff supposed to look real? Because it doesn't. It really doesn't.

Looking at the receptionist behind the glass, I asked if I could see Martha Goldstein. She directed me down a long hallway lined with pictures of different varieties of Arizona cactus. The receptionist had informed Martha of my imminent arrival, because when I walked in, she was already smiling like she was looking forward to seeing me.

The office was in pale tones of gray and brown, and felt homey. Her desk was immaculate, her inbox and outbox both empty. There was a picture on her desk, but I couldn't see it. And there were two pictures on the wall of wild horses running. Somewhere I heard that pictures of wild horses mean you are coming into money. I felt richer already.

"Hello, Lorry. To what do I owe the pleasure of your company?"

"I'm not really sure I'm a pleasure, Martha, but I wanted to ask you a question." I looked down; I didn't like asking people for money. That was Eddie's way, not mine. "Well, um, I was wondering if I could possibly have an advance. You see—"

"Petra already told me you were staying at that horrid motel on the other side of the bridge. Yes, of course you can, and I've already arranged for you to stay at our bed and breakfast." She winked at me. "I'll give you a good rate, too!" She reached into her drawer and handed me a check that was already made out to me.

Astonished, I held out my hand to accept it. "Thank you. Really. I appreciate you doing this. Thank you."

"Oh, it's quite all right. I thought you handled yesterday very well. Other people might have run out screaming. You did exactly the right thing."

"Thank you, Martha."

She handed me a slip of paper. "Here is the address to my house. Will you be coming tonight?"

At first I thought I should stay one more night at the motel since I had already paid for it, and then I remembered the cockroach. And the towels. And the microwave. "Yes!" I said. "Definitely yes. That's all right, isn't it?"

"It's perfectly fine. As I said, I've already arranged it."

"Okay, well, I better get to work now. Thank you so much, Martha. I guess I'll see you later." When I started walking out the door, she called me back.

"Listen, Lorry. I know that Petra looks and sometimes acts a little strange. But don't judge her by that. She's had a hard time of it, and she's very reliable. I can always count on Petra to do the right thing. So don't underestimate her."

Forcing a smile, I said, "Okay, thanks for telling me. I won't. Bye." As I left her office, I wondered if kaleidoscope girl was so reliable, then where was she yesterday morning? She was still on the top of my list of suspects for the murder of that poor woman. Well, she was the only suspect on my list, but who's counting?

CHAPTER EIGHT

I PARKED ON the side street by Johansen's Hardware. As I locked the car and started walking to the corner, I saw a six-foot man in his twenties, with blond hair and blue eyes, checking the cars. It must be old man Johansen's grandson. More power to him.

My mind and eyes were on the man, and I almost missed the little bird at my feet. It had hardly any feathers and wasn't hopping, just shivering. To my right, was a square of earth surrounded by cement, with a fifteen foot tree in the middle of it. On a low branch, was a bird nest with two other little babies in it with their mouths open. The mother bird could have chosen a better place to put her nest, but if she had done that, I wouldn't have been able to return her baby. I picked up the little one and gently put it back in the nest. Mother birds don't recognize their babies by scent, and it's a myth that they will abandon the baby if touched by humans. To prove my words, as I walked away, I looked back over my shoulder to see the mother bird feeding all three of her babies. She didn't even know he was missing, so wasn't surprised when he was back. The "reunion" made me smile.

The sky over the historical society building had a few puffs of white clouds. But oh, did that building ever look impressive. If it wasn't for the bright yellow Koffee Korner, it would be the most beautiful building in town. So instead, that honor went to the post office farther down the block. The post office was a three-story building—one of the oldest buildings in town—with three entrances, all double doors trimmed in white. Only one of the sets of doors opened at any one time, and it was always the center set. The other two sets of doors never opened. Each set of doors had a rounded top comprised of small egg-shaped glass. The windows on the first story had the same pattern. While the first story was built with large beige bricks, with the same egg-shape design over the windows and doors, the rest of the building was red brick with beige columns between the large square windows. Between the first story and the second story, above the center door, were the words, *Rutledge, Arizona* in raised letters. The post office only utilized the first floor. The second floor was the Rutledge Court system, including the court and several official offices, and the third floor was all outside lawyers' offices.

When I entered the historical society and the bell jingled, Petra said, "Can I help you?" from the back, and then when she saw me, she said, "Oh! Hi, Lorry! Where'd you park? There's parking in the back. I thought you knew."

"No one told me. But I understand—everything hasn't been exactly normal around here. My car is across the street, and I could use the exercise anyway."

"Oh! You're not parked in Johansen's parking lot, are you? He walks that lot several times a day and has cars towed away!'"

"As his grandfather did before him!'"

"Well, come on, then. I'll give you a key and show you the back door and where to park." She handed me a key, but as we walked toward the back, the bell jingled as the door opened.

"I'll get it." I walked out to the front to see an older man standing there in a dark blue suit, with a dark blue tie. He was attractive for his age, with salt and pepper hair, and sad-looking eyes. Smiling at him, I asked, "Can I help you?"

"Yes, I'm Michael Wellesley. I've just come from my sister's house, but she doesn't seem to be there. I thought maybe she'd be here."

As I was about to tell him that I didn't have a clue who his sister was, Petra rushed into the room. "Mr. Wellesley, why don't you come to my office back here and sit down?" As he walked past me, she leaned over and whispered, "Call Martha and tell her to come over here immediately! It's urgent!"

When I reached Martha, I told her Petra said it was urgent when a Michael Wellesley walked in. All Martha said besides goodbye, was that she would be right over. Her voice sounded so tense that suddenly I knew exactly who Michael Wellesley was and who his sister, or rather his sisters, were. He was the brother of the two dead women. Oh, dear. Michael and Petra were making small talk in her office, and two minutes later, Martha breezed in and joined them.

"Hello, Michael. Sorry to keep you waiting," Martha said.

"If she's not here, why didn't someone just tell me that
—"

39

Then Petra walked in and stood by my desk, so I couldn't hear anything more of the hushed conversation. "You didn't know who that was, did you?"

I nodded my head. "I do, now."

"How did you know the number for the Town?"

Pointing to the blotter on the desk, I said, "Right here."

"There are dozens of numbers on there! How did you know which was the correct one?"

"It was obvious. All the numbers are written in one hand—I figured that was Betty's"—I whispered the name—"and this one"—I pointed to the number—"was written in another hand. I figured it was yours."

Petra stood there shaking her head with her mouth hanging wide open. I shrugged. "Better close your mouth or you'll catch flies," I said.

She closed her mouth and said, "What else?"

"What do you mean 'what else?'"

"I mean that was a great deduction! Either that or you got lucky. Have you discovered anything else?"

"Oh, you mean about this place?" When she nodded, I went on. "Betty was left-handed. Not only was that bottom drawer empty—for her purse, I assume—but the computer tower is on the left"—I glanced over to the computer—"and the mouse is, too, now that I look at it. It's all a matter of feng shui—everything is at the easiest place possible."

"You're right! She was left-handed! That's amazing! You're as good as Sherlock!"

"Sherlock?"

"You know! Holmes! Sherlock Holmes!"

I gave a quick wave of my hand. "Oh, it's nothing, just a little logic. If I were really good, I would have realized the little water bowl in the bathroom was for an animal!" I scowled.

As if on cue, Rocky, the aforementioned animal, came strolling in as if he owned the joint. He jumped onto my desk, swished his tail in my face just because he could, and then jumped into Petra's arms. My eyes watered and itched, and I sneezed.

Just then, Michael Wellesley emerged from Petra's office, sniffling and dabbing his eyes with his handkerchief. He was about to walk out the door when he noticed Petra holding Rocky. Michael stopped, patted the cat's head, and then proceeded out the door.

Martha came out of the room then, also sniffling and dabbing her eyes with a tissue. "That wasn't easy. He came to arrange one funeral, and now he has to arrange two. They were his only family. And now he has to go to see Sheriff Billy to find out when they'll release the body. So sad. Poor man was distraught."

It hit me at that moment. Was he *really* distraught, or was he pretending? It made me wonder if the two sisters had large life insurance policies.

CHAPTER NINE

AFTER PETRA LEFT for school and Martha returned
to the Town Offices, since I didn't know how soon Petra
could explain all the exhibits to me, I decided that I
should take a look for myself. I had to step over the taped
outline of the dead body on the floor, and I grimaced to
think what if Michael Wellesley had had to go to the
bathroom. I'd have to call Sheriff Billy to ask if I could
remove it. There was also black powder everywhere from
the twelve-year-old forensic team dusting for fingerprints.
I'd have to clean all that off, too.

The big room, beyond the taped outline on the floor,
had what appeared to be three entrances. One to the left
with exhibits, the center one with exhibits, and another
entrance to my right that had a chain pulled across it
with a sign that said *No Admittance*. I assumed since I
worked there that I had permission, but I thought I'd ask
first. You know what assume does. Although I did see
that the forensic boys had been in there with their dust.

I stepped to the left. The first exhibit showed a picture
of a one-room schoolhouse that I remembered seeing
pictures of before. It was the first school in what was

then East Rutledge and had been torn down—or fallen down—nearly a hundred years ago. There were a couple of school desks there and a blackboard. Two plus two equals four was scrawled on it with yellow chalk. In the narrow tray at the bottom of the blackboard sat the chalk eraser.

The next exhibit consisted of clothes from the 1800s. There stood a family of mannikins dressed in nineteenth-century attire. The father wore a vest, purple velvet waistcoat, black patent leather shoes, and a topcoat. The mother wore a purple velvet layered dress with fan-front bodice and a full petticoat underneath. She had on a simple hat tied under her chin, and her feet were hidden beneath the length of the dress. The little girl wore a hoop skirt, a puffy-sleeved blouse with a white lace collar, and a bonnet. On her feet were a pair of Mary Janes. I used to have a pair just like them. And the little boy wore a jacket and skirt—yes, a skirt. I had read in the exhibit documentation that little boys dressed like that until they were five years old. A headless mannikin in the exhibit sported a black lace corset.

The following exhibit was for Grizelda's Bar. It was still in town but currently known as Grizelda's Bar and Grill. When I was in high school, it was briefly called Grizelda's Pizza Parlor. I was in there one time with some friends and got kicked out for laughing too loud. Of course that was pre-Eddie. Because post-Eddie, I had nothing to laugh about. I had plenty to cry about, however.

When I think about giving him the money to pay the mortgage, even knowing that I couldn't trust him with money, I almost think that I set the whole thing up. It was like I was waiting for something so big that even I couldn't ignore it and would *have* to leave him. In a way, I think he knew that. And if I think back on why I even got to that point after putting up with years of his gambling and running around on me with other women, I think it started when he made me give up Bingo.

That little dog, a Cavalier King Charles Spaniel, was my heart and soul. Losing him devastated me. And yet, I had to admit that I went along with it. First it was Eddie telling me to let the neighbors take care of him while we went to Laughlin. That escalated into letting the neighbors keep him permanently. At first I would visit Bingo all the time. And then the neighbors moved to Phoenix and that was the end of that. I went along with it, and yet, it was something I would never forgive Eddie for. The truth was that I hated him. What scared me, though, was that each of the other times we had broken up I had hated him then, too. And yet, I always went back.

Before I had a chance to peruse the Grizelda exhibit, the phone rang and I hurried to my desk to answer it. "Rutledge Historical Society. May I help you? . . . Yes, hi, Martha. . . . Of course. No problem. . . . I'm sorry, I haven't seen the printer. . . . Okay, I can do that. I'll get on it right away. . . .Yes, I have it written down. . . . All right. I'll tell her when she comes back in. . . . You're welcome. Goodbye."

I sat down at my desk and flicked the computer on. While it started up, I opened the file drawer in the desk and searched through the files for one labeled To Be Typed. After I found it, I looked through the file. There were two handwritten papers in there; I selected the second one, and started typing it up using Word. It didn't take too long to finish typing and proofreading it, and then I opened my personal gmail account, attached the file to an email, and sent it off to Martha.

It was almost time for Petra to return from school. I sat back in the chair thinking back on Eddie again. He really was a horrible person, but he had *always* been a horrible person, and I had married him anyway. The *why* is what bothered me. Whatever. I was grateful that I had the courage to walk away—or drive away—and even more grateful that he had no idea where I was.

I heard the bell jingle and the door open, and guess who walked in. Yup, that's right. Fast Eddie. In the flesh.

CHAPTER TEN

THERE HE STOOD, with freshly pressed slacks, new, a blue sweater that showed off his slender build and his non-existent muscles, new, and spit-polished black shoes. Eddie always was a sharp dresser. It was one of the things I had always loved about him.

"Hiya, Truck!" He smiled his beguiling smile at me. Glancing to my right, he said, "I see that you have your beloved fish tank back. I can't stand those things." He sniffed. "They stink and make noise." He focused his attention on me and took a step closer. "Aren't you glad to see me?"

"No, Eddie, I'm not. How did you find me?"

"I can always find you, Darling." He took a step closer and put his hand over his heart. "My heart leads me straight to you."

Can you believe I used to fall for lines like that? "Get off it, Eddie. What do you want?"

"You know what I want, Lorry. I want to get back together with you—where we belong."

I hadn't expected that. And it wasn't just the slick lines that had gotten to me in the past, it was that he *wanted* me. Sensing I was weakening, Eddie went in for the kill.

"Come on, Lorry. Let me take you out for dinner tonight. You know we belong together." He reached out for my hand. I didn't give it to him.

The bell jingled on the door, and Petra came in for her afternoon shift. She looked at me and at Eddie reaching for my hand, and then she shook her head and walked into her office. Her presence made me feel stronger.

"Eddie, what happened to the money I gave you for the mortgage? My house was foreclosed! I loved that house."

"*Our* house, baby. Community property state, remember?"

"Forget that, Eddie! What *happened* to the money I gave you every month to pay the mortgage?"

"I invested it in something way more valuable than that house, baby." He leaned closer to me. "I'm onto something so big that we'll be rich beyond your wildest dreams!" He smiled his disarming smile.

Surprisingly, it didn't get to me. "I *loved* that house, Eddie. And *you* lost it for me! I'm staying in a crummy motel over the bridge! Where are you staying?"

"Listen, Truck, I need to leave right now. I have an appointment. Can you loan me a few bucks? This thing will hit big real soon, but I need something to carry me over until then. You can trust me. I'll pay you back as soon as it hits." Something distracted him. He kept glancing out the window. I looked out. There was a dirty white pickup parked in front. Definitely not Eddie's style.

The check Martha had given me felt like it was vibrating in my pocket, but I wasn't going to give it up. "No, Eddie, I'm sorry. I have no money. You should know that—you cleaned out both accounts before our trip to the Grand Canyon. Very slick. You're on your own now. Leave me alone."

Catching me unawares, he reached out again and grabbed my hand. "Baby," he crooned, "we belong together. You know we do. We can do great things together." He leaned forward toward me, but I saw his eyes sweep to the side again.

I moved away from him. "Eddie, get out of here! I have no money, and I'm not interested in you or your big plans! Get out!" Technically, I wasn't lying. While I did have the *check* in my pocket, I had no *cash money*.

He straightened up, shrugged his shoulders, and opened the door. Before he stepped out onto the street, he poked his head around and said, "I'll be back, Truck. We belong together." I wanted to watch what car he got into, but Petra chose that moment to come in.

"Truck? That's a peculiar pet name. What's that from?"

I frowned. It was a name he had called me for years. And although I didn't like it, like the rest of Eddie's crap, I let it go. "In England, they call a big truck a lorry. My name is Lorry. Therefore, he calls me Truck."

"That's insulting!"

She was right. I didn't look at her.

"And you know he was with another woman!"

"How could you possibly know that?" I wanted to know.

"Look! In that classic red mustang! He hasn't driven away yet!" She pointed out the window.

In front of the dirty white pickup, the mustang hesitated before pulling into traffic, with Eddie driving, and a blond bombshell in the passenger seat. Although I couldn't tell from the back of her that she was a bombshell, that was Eddie's type. And she even looked familiar. I bit my lip and shook my head.

"You're not going back to that jerk, are you?"

I looked up at her with tears starting to seep from my eyes. Quietly, I said, "I usually do."

"Lorry! I don't even know you, but I know you deserve better than that jerk!" She looked out the window. "Okay. He's driving that red mustang, and what are you driving? That old Karmann Ghia across the street?"

The door had opened before she finished the question, and Kasey walked in. "Was that Eddie in that red mustang? With a *girl?*" Before I had a chance to answer, she added, "And what did he want?" Not waiting for an answer to that question, either, Kasey asked another. "And you're driving an old Karmann Ghia now? What happened to that nice Taurus you had?"

"That jerk probably sold it for the investment deal of a lifetime!" chimed in Petra.

"No. He wrecked it driving drunk coming home from the casino one night after he lost."

Petra made a motion mimicking hitting herself in the head. "Even worse! What were you doing with that jerk in the first place?"

"She loved him," said Kasey quietly.

"The question is, why?" Petra stepped closer to me and shook her finger in my face. "Tell me that you're not going back to that jerk!"

"You're not going back to him *again*, are you, Lorry?" asked Kasey incredulously.

"No! She's not! And we will not let her!" Petra said, with Kasey nodding her head in agreement. "What you need," said Petra, "is more self-esteem. If you liked yourself better, you wouldn't even *consider* a cad like that!"

"I like myself just fine!" I crossed my arms over my chest.

Kasey tilted her head to look at me, put her hand on my shoulder, and said, "Then why do you let him treat you so badly? Have you forgotten what happened with Bingo?"

"Forget about Bingo!" I said, more loudly than I meant. The two women stepped back in surprise. "Okay then! How can I get more self-esteem?"

Petra thought for a minute. She looked up at the ceiling, and her eyes traveled back and forth. "I've got it! You're so good at making deductions, *you're* going to solve Gwen's murder!"

I wanted to say no, that's a silly idea. But the idea appealed to me. Wasn't I already thinking about suspects? The trouble was, number one on my suspect list was Petra. Although it didn't make sense that she would ask me to solve the murder if she was the perp. Maybe I was wrong about her. Today, she even wore some respectable clothing—matching blouse and decent length skirt—and they even covered up her tattoos. Of course, they couldn't cover her piercings, but at least she was halfway there.

CHAPTER ELEVEN

KASEY LEFT AND Petra led me back to where I had found the body. "Let's start here. Where do you think the killer was and what was the murder weapon?"

"Doesn't Sheriff Billy already have the murder weapon?" I didn't know, but I had assumed that he had. Again that shows what assume does.

"No, he doesn't. He said that there was a head injury, but he hadn't found the murder weapon. I asked him."

"Oh, are you on a *personal basis* with Sheriff Billy? Perhaps because you've visited his jail?" I asked it as a wisecrack, but truth was, I wanted to know.

"No!" she said indignantly, but her face turned red. "He's a friend!"

I held up my hands in defeat. "Okay, okay."

"Do you want to do this or not?" she demanded.

"Yes, I do. I'm sorry."

"All right. You can see where the forensic guys dusted for fingerprints. Maybe you can find some information from that. Martha was planning on having someone come in to clean it all up. I'll ask her to wait."

"Why don't you tell her to forget about someone else

cleaning it? I'll do it myself, that way I can study everything as I clean."

"Great idea!"

"How about this no admittance area? Can I go in there?"

Petra undid the chain and walked in. "Of course! That's so nobody goes out the back door."

"Oh, yeah. You never showed me. Where's the back door?" I asked as I followed Petra's example of stepping over a box of binders in the way. Its contents looked as if they were thrown in the box any which way. As we walked toward the back, there were several more boxes of binders lined up against the wall. The binders in those boxes were neat and orderly.

"Let me show you the door and where to park, too."

Petra led the way through the narrow passageway until we came to two doors. She opened the one that led to the parking lot in back. "Here," she said. "Park anywhere to my right. There are always spaces here."

"Where's your car?"

She shrugged. "I take the bus."

That would make sense since she always came in through the front door. Petra turned around to lead me back through the passageway, but I stopped her. "What's that other door?"

"Oh! That's a door to the Koffee Korner. It's never used."

It struck me as curious. "Wait a second. Look at this, Petra. There's no fingerprint dust here." I pointed to the back door. "What if they came in that way?"

"You're right! See! I told you that you could do this!" She clapped her hands together. "See! You've discovered something already!"

"Well, it's not for sure the perp"—since I was now "officially" investigating a crime scene, I figured it would be okay to use that word—"used this door, but it should have been considered."

"You're right. Sheriff Billy might not even know about this entrance. I'll let him know."

"Cops are so arrogant. Won't he disparage you if you point out what he might have missed?"

"Lorry! Where do you get these ideas about cops? From that creep of an ex-husband of yours? Billy is a kind, funny, generous man. If he thinks it's valid, he'll send the guys back over here."

"Yeah, I'll bet."

She stood there with her hands on her hips. "You know what, Lorry? You're judging people and things from your *ex*-husband's point of view. It's just like the fish tank. You said you hated them because he does, but the truth is that you really like them. You need to get over that, girlfriend!"

I would have liked to slap the impudent little kaleidoscope girl across the face, except she was exactly right. So in reality, I should slap my own face instead. For years, I had adopted Eddie's likes and dislikes, his prejudices, and his assumptions. I had completely lost myself somewhere along the way. "I'll try," I said in a soft voice, not quite a whisper.

"Come on, let me show you the upstairs. You're going to have to start doing some work up there, anyway. That's what Betty was doing before—you know."

Following her up the stairs, I noticed there was a hand-railing and the steps felt secure. We got to the top, and I looked around. Large bookshelves lined the walls, and there were library-type bookshelves through half the room. I heard a meow and looked up. Rocky the cat was there, stretching. Next thing I knew, he came flying down and landed in Petra's arms. She kissed him on the top of his head.

"He's not going to do that to me, is he?" I sneezed.

"No, I taught him that. He only does that to me. But he likes it up here and hangs out here most of the time on the top shelves. Usually, unless he stands up, you can't even see him."

"What's all this stuff doing up here, anyway?"

"It's getting organized so we can scan it all and put it online. That's what all the historical societies are doing nowadays. Give the public better access. Plus, this was all downstairs before we enlarged the exhibit area." She started down the stairs. "Okay, now that you've had your tour, I need to get to work."

As I stood at the top of the stairs, I tried to imagine Betty carrying that big box of books upstairs. "Petra?"

She had already reached the bottom of the stairs, but she turned around. "Yes?"

"Betty was older, right?"

"Yeah, she was really old. Sixty-five or seventy. She worked here because she always had, and she loved the place."

"That wasn't my point. What was a seventy-year-old woman doing carrying up a big box of books like that? How could she even be that strong? They look heavy."

Petra nodded her head. "You're right. Usually she just carried up a few binders at a time."

"You said 'usually.' You mean sometimes she *did* carry the whole box of 'em up?"

"No, that was a mistake. I never saw her carry a whole box up. I *always* saw her carry just a few binders up." She started back toward her desk and then returned to the stairs just as I reached the bottom. "See that! You're right again! That's the second thing you've discovered!" She patted me on the shoulder. "Way to go, girl!"

CHAPTER TWELVE

I HAD TO admit that her words made me feel good—even if they came from a sixteen-year-old kaleidoscope girl. Maybe I did need some self-esteem. It was for sure I never got any from Eddie. He always made me feel bad about myself. Calling me Truck for one. And all the things he did that I went along with kind of chipped away at my self-esteem and self-confidence a little at a time. Until there was none.

When I got back to my desk and sat down, the phone immediately rang. It was Martha. "Yes, Martha, hello. . . . Really? Are you sure? . . . Okay, then. I will. *Thank you* very much! I really appreciate it. . . . See you soon, then. Bye."

Martha wanted me to leave to pack up my belongings at the motel so I wouldn't have to spend another night there. What a sweet woman she was. Maybe my life was looking up at last. Martha treated me like a decent human being. Not that Joe McDonald had treated me badly. But the last few years, he hadn't spent much time in the office anyway. And toward the end there, I was beginning to suspect he was getting dementia. He kept to himself and only talked to me when he needed something typed.

"Petra!" I called as I pulled my purse out of the drawer. "Martha called and said I should leave so I can move my stuff over to her house." I walked to the edge of the door so I could see her. "So I'll see you tomorrow."

"Okay, see you tomorrow, then."

Something occurred to me, so before I reached the outside door, I turned back. "Petra, the phone hasn't rung all day. Is that normal?"

Petra nodded. "Sometimes it is. Sometimes it rings off the hook, and other times it doesn't ring for days. It's fine. Don't worry about it. Bye." She turned back to her work and then looked up again before I had a chance to walk away. "We normally get local business—people wanting to look at the exhibits and the genealogical information—but I honestly think the locals are kind of freaked out over two people dying here within a few days. They don't want to come in. But I think they'll get over it in a week or two. Don't worry about it." Then without saying another word, she started typing on her keyboard.

The West Rutledge Motel did have a laundry room, so when I got there, I put everything in it that could be washed—which was almost everything—and then returned to my room to pack. After what Petra said about bedbugs, and after seeing the cockroach that morning, I didn't want to take a chance of bringing anything bad over to Martha's. It wouldn't take long, anyway. Everything else in the room that I couldn't wash got a careful going over to check for any rude little critters before it made it into my car. The dresses that had been hanging in the closet opposite the lavatory got an especially good going over. I checked every seam, every button and buttonhole, and I even ran my hand along each hem to make sure nothing had crawled between the stitches.

Yes, everything would fit in my tiny Karmann Ghia. Most of my belongings were at a storage unit that I had paid for with my one unemployment check. Now that I thought of it, I took out my cell phone to call the unemployment office and tell them that I had gotten work. The cell phone was nearly dead. I had just enough battery left to make the call. The thing hadn't rung in days—well, since the call from Martha telling me I had gotten the job—and so I hadn't bothered to charge it.

I walked to the motel laundry to move the clothes into the dryer. The dryers there worked exceedingly well. They didn't look new, but they certainly had the power to get most loads dry in thirty minutes. Putting the last few items in the car to organize them better, I spent the remaining time going over every inch of my suitcases for any living thing that didn't belong there. No living thing belonged there ever, but you know what I mean. Then I put the empty suitcases in the car. I wasn't going to take a chance on taking the laundry into the room and having something untoward jumping into the suitcases before I moved them to the car.

So when the laundry was finished, I took said clothes directly to the car, folded them carefully, and placed them into the suitcase. The dresses hung on the hooks by the backs of the seats. Hopefully, they wouldn't get wrinkled. It was only a few minutes back to Rutledge and Martha's house.

After checking out of the motel and the owner trying

to tell me that I had paid through the following day and didn't have to leave yet, I bid him adieu, and slid behind the wheel of my car. Closing my eyes, I thanked my lucky stars that nothing bad had happened to me while I stayed at that motel. It was in a bad part of town, but no one had broken into my room or my crummy old car. They probably figured that anybody who owned a car like that needed the stuff worse than they did. I started the car and drove over the bridge for a final time. Goodbye West Rutledge Motel, goodbye Coyote Moon, goodbye Eddie, and hello new and auspicious life. At least I hoped it would be.

CHAPTER THIRTEEN

I CROSSED THE river, drove past High Street where the historical society was, drove past Main Street where the sheriff's station and the Town Offices were, drove past Commercial Avenue where there was a tire store, an auto parts store, and other fringe commercial endeavors, and headed toward the residential area of town. I turned right on Meadowside Lane, Martha's street. If I had turned left, I would have turned on Hillside Terrace, the street where I grew up—in the rich side of town, where the *mansions* were.

Martha's Bed and Breakfast, called that even though her husband ran it while she worked, was located at the end of the street by the meadow. It was a beautiful, tall blue and gray Victorian. The right side of the house, slightly shorter than the left, had two windows on the bottom floor and one window on the second floor. On the left side of the house, taller and wider than the right, there was one arched window that looked like it belonged in a church, with a smaller rectangular window on either side of it. The second floor on that side had the same setup and the same size windows. Between the two sides of the house, the front door had the same arched door as the windows on the left. And above it stood a tower that rose two stories high and had the same arched window with a small balcony that may or may not have been viable. It was too small to even put a chair on, so it might have been just for show.

I loved Victorians because I grew up in one. Ours was huge, with servants' quarters in the rear, in which lived real live servants. My family was rich. When my father died when I was ten, my mother remarried twice to even richer men. Why couldn't I have followed her lead? Come to think of it, why didn't I listen to her? She hated Eddie and often told me what a loser he was. And then when I married him, she—oh it's too terrible to even think about what she did.

A double garage stood to the right of the house, and since it was late enough that Martha should be at home, I pulled into the driveway so it would be easier for me to unload. I picked up the clothes hanging on each side of the car, and I rang the doorbell.

A short man, about as round as he was tall, opened the door. Almost completely bald, he had a few strands of hair combed over the top. He wore a dark green sweatsuit and had a huge grin on his face. "You must be Lorry! Come on in!" He opened the door for me, and I strolled in.

Then Martha came running in from the kitchen. She wore jeans and a sweatshirt and had a red checked apron over it. "Welcome, Lorry! This is my husband, Hugo." Hugo nodded to Lorry. "Come on, now. Let me show you to your room. It's right up this way." She led the way up a beautiful wide staircase with a walnut handrail. It was so beautiful and shiny that I hesitated to touch it.

Oh, wait. I couldn't touch it. I had both hands full.

Struggling to see the stair in front of me because of what I was carrying, I made it to the top of the stairs. The upstairs was painted a light blue, a shade lighter than the outside of the house.

"Our room is on this side of the house, and your room is on the other side. Your room is the only other room up here that has its own bathroom. Luckily, the people who were in it checked out this morning."

When she opened the door to my room, its beauty impressed me. Painted in pastel yellow and green, it had a picture of the ocean over the bed. And out through the window, I could see the meadow. The bed, a four-poster pineapple bed—the kind with pineapples on the top of the posts—had a heavy print bedspread that matched the walls. The room was immaculate. Martha opened the door to the closet, and I hung up the clothes I had brought up with me.

"Lorry, I'm sorry that we can't help you carry your belongings in. Hugo has a sore back, and I'm in the middle of dinner. He usually does the cooking during the week, but he's been gone most of the day."

"No problem, Martha. I don't have that much, anyway. And I'm grateful that you're even letting me stay here. It is a hundred percent turnaround from where I've been staying!"

Martha nodded and hurried down the stairs. Then she turned around. I had just gotten to the top of the stairs myself. "Lorry, we would like you to eat dinner with us tonight. I'm sure with packing and moving and all, you haven't had time to get anything."

"Oh, no. I can't put you to the trouble," I said, hoping that she would try to convince me. It smelled delicious.

"No trouble! I'll set a place for you." And with that it was decided, and she disappeared through the door.

CHAPTER FOURTEEN

BY THE TIME I finished unloading the car, dinner was about to start. As I put the last load into my room upstairs, I heard Hugo singing in the kitchen. "Dinner is almost ready to be served! Come join us at the table and don't be reserved!" He was off-key but sincere. I rushed down, so as not to keep them waiting.

The kitchen was large with modern appliances, which made a nice contrast to all the antiques in the house. Dinner was served at an octagonal wormwood table. If you don't know what wormwood is, it's a type of wood with little holes in it that looks like it has been attacked by killer worms. I don't know about you, but I don't like to think about worms while I'm eating. Luckily, woven placemats covered the table in front of my eyes. So if I really tried, I could avoid thinking about worms. I really tried.

Martha was sitting at the table when I walked in, and Hugo had the apron on and was serving dinner. He placed a big platter of fried chicken at the table, followed by mashed potatoes, fresh peas, and a big salad bowl. Who eats fried chicken in these days of high cholesterol and high blood pressure? No wonder Hugo was as round as he was tall, and Martha was no skinny-minny, either. Come to think of it, neither was I. Since fried chicken was one of my favorites that I didn't allow myself too often, I dug right in.

Dinner conversation consisted of Hugo's tales—tall or not—of his adventures in the navy. One time a torpedo narrowly missed the ship he was on. When they returned fire, they hit the other ship and blew it to smithereens. At that point, he broke into off-key song again. "We hit that there ship and blew her away! Now it won't come back another day!" I cracked up at his singing. Martha looked at him with love in her eyes. And when he finished singing, Hugo sat up a little straighter and looked back at her the same way. Oh, what I would give to have a love like that.

Dinner wouldn't be complete without dessert, and so when we finished dinner and the table was cleared, Hugo brought out an apple pie and vanilla ice cream. It must have been yesterday's pie, because a couple of slices were already missing from it. But Hugo popped three pieces into the microwave and handed them out. Then he passed around the ice cream with a fancy metal ice cream scoop. The rich vanilla ice cream melted over the warm pie, and it was like heaven itself. I felt stuffed.

"Thank you so much for dinner and dessert! It was all delicious!" I stood up and placed my dirty plate into the sink where Hugo had put the rest of the dirty dishes. "I'll help do the dishes."

"Oh, no, missy. You're not taking my job away!" said Hugo, gently pushing me away from the sink. "You're a guest, and besides, you still have some unpacking to do."

"Well, thank you, Hugo. Thank you both again so

much for dinner. I appreciate it."

"No problem, Lorry. Tomorrow, breakfast will be at seven o'clock. See you then!"

I smiled and nodded and then stumbled up the stairs. It had been a long day both emotionally and physically, what with seeing Eddie and then packing and unpacking. All I wanted to do was sit in bed and read and then go to sleep. But all I had done so far was retrieve my stuff from my car. I still had to put it all away. When I opened the door of my room and saw all that stuff on my bed, I just wanted to sit down and weep. That happened to me sometimes after an emotional day. It's like the emotions had taken everything out of me that I had to give, and I had nothing left to deal with stress. And when you were as tired as I felt, any kind of stress was too much stress.

So I sat on the edge of the bed—the only place that had no stuff on it—and I put my hands over my face. Then I clicked my heels together and said aloud, "There's no place like home. There's no place like home." It didn't work, though, probably because they weren't ruby slippers. My home—the one Eddie and I had shared for years—was gone for good, and here I was living at a bed and breakfast. It was several steps above the West Rutledge Motel, but it wasn't *my* home. And I so wanted *mine*.

CHAPTER FIFTEEN

BEFORE IT WAS even nine o'clock, I had already slipped into bed. I had put all my clothes away in the antique dresser, I had sat on each of the two antique chairs in the room—they were both more beautiful than comfortable—and then I had taken a leisurely bath in the antique claw-foot bathtub. It was heavenly. The bed felt comfortable. It had one of those pillow-top mattresses. And I fell asleep listening to coyote song from a pack that were in the meadow outside my windows. Life was good.

The next morning I got dressed and bounded down the stairs to the smell of breakfast. Hugo had on the apron again, and Martha sat at the already set table. "Good morning!" she said when she saw me.

"Good morning, Martha, Hugo!"

"Did you sleep well?" Martha asked.

"I slept wonderfully. It felt so good to fall asleep to the sound of coyotes. I haven't done that for years. When I was a kid, I loved that sound. Still do."

"Oh, that's right. You used to live—"

"Yes, over on Hillside Terrace."

Hugo turned around and raised his eyebrows but said nothing. Martha just nodded.

Breakfast consisted of scrambled eggs, bacon, English muffins, and real butter. At least they'd given up margarine with its trans-fatty acids. That was a step in the right direction. Martha asked if I wanted pink grapefruit juice or orange juice. I chose the orange juice, and it turned out to be fresh-squeezed. Breakfast was as delicious as dinner the night before. But maybe I could buy cereal and milk to have the following day. I can't be eating a cholesterol disaster like this every day. I have to mind my girlish figure. Or something.

Martha finished and left the house before me, and then I finished. I thanked Hugo for the delicious meal and walked upstairs to powder my nose. When I finished the powdering, I walked downstairs and out the door to my car. The keys! I had forgotten my keys—and my purse—upstairs. Sometimes I think I'd forget my head if it—well, forget that. When I walked downstairs again, Hugo was on the other side of the house. When he saw me, he said, "Can't make up your mind if you're coming or going?"

"No, it's not that, Hugo. I'm trying to work off that delicious breakfast you cooked me!" I smiled at him.

He patted his big stomach. "I guess I could use some of that, too."

When I got into my car and tried to start it, the engine didn't want to turn over. After trying several more times, smelling the fumes of gasoline, and fearing that I'd flooded the engine, it made one last gasp and started. My Taurus was such a great car. I missed it. And I missed the house. And most of all I missed Bingo. And every one of those things I had lost because of Eddie. Yes, I allowed it all to happen, but—okay, face it, Lorry. There is no but. He did it, but you let him. Face it and move on. It's all in the past. Nothing like a little tough-love self-talk to get you going in the morning. Or get you crying. One of the two. Maybe both.

Instead of going directly to the historical society to start work, I made a quick stop at the bank to cash my check. Two hundred dollars. I would give it all to Martha for my board and room.

I parked in the back of the historical society where Petra had showed me. Using the key she had given me, I walked inside and retraced my steps from the day before. The passage went behind the exhibits. I walked past the row of boxes and stepped over the one by the dead-body outline on the floor. Then I sneezed, rubbed my itchy eyes, and cursed the dratted cat.

Petra heard my footsteps—and my sneeze. She called out from her office. "Lorry? Is that you? I think I'd recognize those heels anywhere!"

I chuckled. "Yes, Petra, it's me."

"I have a message for you. It was taped to the door."

"Who would leave me a message?" I asked as I put my purse into the bottom drawer of my desk. And then, in a second, I had a chill over my whole body because I knew exactly who it was. It could have been Martha, but it wasn't. I was certain of that. Walking into Petra's office with a frown on my face, I said, "It was him, wasn't it?"

Petra nodded with the same frown on her face. "He really is a jerk, isn't he?" She picked up a piece of paper in front of her and began reading it aloud. "Checked with the West Rutledge Motel, and they said you checked out. So I figured you must have come into some cash. I'd like to share. We're still a team. Love, Eddie."

I took a deep breath, closed my eyes, and made a decision: I was getting a divorce. I was officially done with Fast Eddie. Once and for all. When I turned to go, Petra called me back.

"There's a PS," she said. "I'll be back later to pick up the money."

Closing my eyes again, I said slowly through clenched teeth, "I'm filing for divorce."

Petra smiled. "I had a feeling you'd say that. So I printed these up for you." She handed me a bunch of papers. "Divorce. From old French, meaning to separate, leave one's husband, turn aside."

After rolling my eyes and snorting, I thought, yup, time to turn aside, and then I said, "What are these?"

"Forms for your divorce. You don't have to go to some fancy attorney. You can do it yourself, and it hardly costs anything. Just a few hundred dollars, usually."

I took the forms from her and leafed through them, shaking my head. "Thanks so much, Petra, but I can't do it. At least not right now."

"Why not?"

"I don't have any extra money right now. I'm paying Martha rent with the money she advanced me."

Petra knotted her brows. "I'll see if I can figure something out."

For a murder suspect, she certainly was accommodating.

CHAPTER SIXTEEN

SITTING DOWN AT my desk, I shuffled through the forms. "It will take me a while to go through these. I couldn't have filed today, anyway."

Petra stepped into the office. Today she was wearing jeans with rips all over the thigh portion of the leg. Her t-shirt had rips in the middle of it, again exposing her bellybutton ring. Forgetting about that, what was with teens today? Or I should say, what's with fashion for teens today? Between boys wearing their pants halfway down their bum and girls wearing pre-torn clothing because it's in style, it's crazy. Of course, who am I to talk? I adjusted my high heel. Whoever invented those stupid things should be hung! And yet, they were all I ever wore.

"I called Sheriff Billy this morning and told him about the back door. He had his boys come out first thing and dust our back door, the door between us and Koffee Korner, and the back door into Koffee Korner. I also told him you were working on the case."

"I bet he was thrilled to hear that."

"I heard the smile in his voice when he said, 'We'll

see.'"

"What's *that* supposed to mean?" I asked.

She shrugged. "Don't know. I would've filled out the forms for you, but I didn't know your maiden name."

"Lockharte *is* my maiden name. Eddie took many things from me, but for some reason I wouldn't let that go. Probably because I like alliteration."

Petra looked at the ceiling again, her eyes roaming from side to side. "Your maiden name is Lockharte, and you grew up here." Her eyes got big and round. "You're one of the Rutledge Lockhartes?"

I exhaled quickly through my nose, shook my head in disgust, and then said in a soft voice, "Yes."

"Really? A Rutledge Lockharte and you were staying at the West Rutledge Motel? What's *that* about?"

I shook my head. I wasn't going into that now.

"Oh, come on. Tell me!"

Then I got an idea, so I turned toward her and smiled. "So where were you the other morning when you were supposed to be here at work—the day that Gwen was murdered? Come on, tell me where you were."

Petra looked at me, anger springing to her face. She slapped the desk and walked briskly into the other room. I heard her sit down hard with a thud, and then she said nothing for several minutes. When she returned, she had a funny look on her face like she was about to cry.

"All right. I'll tell you—if you tell me."

That request surprised me. I hadn't intended on telling her—or anyone—because I didn't want anyone to know the dirty details. Now I was on the spot. "O-kay," I said, drawing out the word. "You first."

"You promise you'll tell me after?"

Nodding, I said, "Yes, I promise."

"Okay! I was at an interview at school."

"For what? Like a job? Financial aid or something?"

"No! They approached me. The school."

I could tell she was having a hard time with the story. She was blinking back tears. "Go on," I encouraged.

"About going to college in my junior and senior year of high school. I would take the classes online, and when it came time to graduate, if I finished all my classes, I would graduate high school *and* get an AA college degree at the same time."

"Wow! That's great! Then why are you—"

"*Both* my parents had to attend the interview, because I had to get permission from *both* of them." She sniffled. "The meeting was at eight o'clock in the morning. Eight o'clock in the morning and my father was already *drunk*. Or maybe *still* drunk from the night before."

Not knowing what else to say, I shrugged my shoulders and said softly, "At least he showed up."

"Yes, he showed up and signed the documents that needed signing. But he almost didn't sign at all."

"Why not?"

"When he found out how much the college classes cost. I already had the money covered, but he said he didn't want charity. The fool struggled to his feet and almost fell over. And I had to explain that it was a *loan* not charity. Finally, he signed. I was never so humiliated in my whole life." Tears ran down her face, but instead of looking down or trying to hide them, she looked right at me. "Which was so stupid!" she said forcefully. "It's a small town. The whole town *already* knew he was a stinking drunk. Still, it embarrassed me."

Standing up, I put my arms around her and stroked her hair and her back trying to calm her. Surprisingly, she hugged me back. "Thank you, Lorry," she said. She broke away from me. "Okay, now you tell me."

I looked down and nodded my head slowly. "All right. I moved to Coyote Moon and started college there. I'd come home on weekends and everything was fine. And then I met Eddie. My mother didn't like him. More like hated him. She warned me about him. Now I wish that I had listened. Everything she said about him came true: I'd lose my car, I'd lose my home, he'd fool around.

"When I married him, my mother officially disinherited me and cut me out of her will. At least that's what she said, and of course I didn't believe that she'd actually do that. Until she died unexpectedly. And I called the lawyer, and they confirmed it. I didn't get a penny. End of story. That's how I went from a highbrow Lockharte on Hillside Terrace to poor white trash living in the West Rutledge Motel."

"I'm sorry, Lorry. I mean it. I'm really sorry."

"That's okay, Petra. I've come to terms with it over the years. Of course, now that Eddie and I are *going to get a divorce!*—I feel even worse about it. But oh well. I did it for love. Or stupidity. Or something." I thought of something from Petra's story. "Hey, where did you get the loan for college?"

Petra put her hands on her hips. "Billy," she said indignantly.

I blinked and took a step backwards. "Do you and he have, you know, a *thing* going on?"

"Yuck, no! He's thirty-five years old!"

I tilted my head at her. "It wouldn't be unheard of. And he's very attractive."

"Let me tell you something about Billy. He is the most decent, generous human being that I know! I've known him since I was four, when I'd go with my mom to bail my father out of the drunk tank."

"Was he the sheriff then?" That was many years ago, so I had to ask.

"No, just a deputy. But he's seen me grow up, and he's seen what I had to put up with. He's a good guy. He didn't even want to loan me the money, he wanted to *give* it to me. He said that anyone who had to put up with as much as I did deserved a good break, and he was willing to give it to me."

"Wow, I'm impressed." It made me think of something. "Petra, I've done some reading—you know—and I've read where a lot of children of alcoholics end up marrying alcoholics. You won't do that, will you?"

"Absolutely not! My boyfriend doesn't drink at all. And if he started, I'd dump him in an instant. But I know he won't."

"Okay, good. I'm glad to hear that."

She began to return to her office when she turned around and came back. "Lorry, I know you judge me by how I look"—she motioned to her clothes, her tattoos, and her piercings—"but please don't judge me by my father."

I wanted to tell her that I didn't judge her, but I wasn't going to lie. Because I absolutely did judge her by those things. And at that moment, I felt very, very ashamed of it. So I looked down and said, "No, Petra. I promise I won't."

CHAPTER SEVENTEEN

AN HOUR LATER, as Petra was about to leave, she handed me a slip of paper with my new email and password on it. Then she handed me another piece of paper on how to change the password. I looked at the first piece of paper and handed her back the second. "This password that you gave me is fine, Petra. I'll keep it!"

She smiled at me when the bell jingled, the door opened, and Sheriff Billy walked in. Before he could say anything, the piece of paper with my password slipped out of my hand and floated to the floor. He stooped down to pick it up and looked at it.

"Hmmmm. Lorry at Rutledge Historical Society dot com. Password equals No More Eddie!" He handed the paper back to me and said, "That sounds provocative." Petra laughed.

"Hello, Sheriff Billy." I took the paper from him. "Thank you."

"Hello, Lorry," he said with a smile on his face. "Hello, Petra. How's school?" He raised his eyebrows.

Petra smiled at him. "Very good, Billy, very good."

"Is everything going smoothly?"

She nodded. "Very smoothly. Thank you."

He started at that, and I saw his eyes move in my direction and then back to hers with a questioning look. "That's good," he said hesitantly.

"She knows, Billy. We traded secrets today. She won't say anything to anyone."

"You have secrets, then, Lorry Lockharte?"

I tilted my head at him. "*Every* girl has secrets, Sheriff Billy."

He smiled. "Well, I came in to thank you for the information about the back door. That cracked the case for us. So thank you." Billy made a quick bow in my direction.

"You caught who killed Gwen?" I asked.

"Sure did. It was from a print on the door between the cafe and here. Matched it up to someone in our files. A boy by the name of Zackary James. He just got out of jail, and now he's right back in."

With a quick sidelong glance, I saw the color had drained from Petra's face. What was that about?

"Yeah," Billy continued, "he'd been out only two days. We figure that he came in here to steal something, she caught him, and he killed her. Very sad."

"Oh!" said Petra, "I need to get to school before I'm late. See you both later! Bye!"

She walked toward the door, and Billy moved over for her to pass. We both said goodbye to her.

"Well, I guess that's it, Lorry. I just wanted to thank you and let you know that you can stop investigating." He shrugged. "Sorry to spoil your fun!"

"You say he just got out of jail?" I asked.

"Yes, two days ago."

77

"And Betty was found before that, right?"

"Ye-es," he drew out the word so it had two syllables. "What difference does it make? Betty fell down the stairs."

"Petra said that Betty never carried a whole box of books upstairs. It disturbs me that she did that night. Doesn't that seem inconsistent to you?"

"I think she was here alone and trying to save time. And it was a fatal mistake."

"I don't know, Sheriff Billy. It doesn't feel right to me. It doesn't make sense."

He put his hand on my shoulder. "Well, Lorry, since you're new at this, and I'm an experienced law officer with experienced deputies, I think you should leave the crime-solving to us."

"You mean those two twelve-year-olds? How experienced could they be? Besides, how many murders have you had to solve in Rutledge?"

"Not many, but—"

The radio hooked to his shirt squawked, and a voice said, "Sheriff Billy? You there?"

He squeezed the button. "I'm right here. You need me?"

"Yes. Can you come back to the office, please?"

"I'll be right there!" He looked at me, smiled, and said, "Lorry. It's been a pleasure. I'll talk to you later."

I nodded. "Goodbye, Sheriff Billy."

It bothered me. Why would Petra react that way to hearing the name Zackary James? Maybe I could find out later when she came back. I had already discounted her as a suspect when she told me the story about being at school. What if she and Zackary James were in it together? That was a possibility, wasn't it? But then what about Betty? No, that didn't make sense, either. Then why the reaction to his name? It was all so confusing. Should I go down and talk to Zackary James? Oh, it would probably be wiser to speak to Petra first. Now that we had told each other our most intimate secrets, she would probably tell me about him. I'd have to wait until she came in for her afternoon shift.

The phone rang, and it was someone asking if we were now open for business. I said yes, and as I hung up the phone, the bell jingled again, and the door opened.

A tall, handsome man in a gray three-piece suit with a blue tie, walked in. He had kindly blue eyes, and his black hair was graying at the temples. His shoes were shined to a mirror-finish. In a word, he was gorgeous. I was so overwhelmed at his appearance, I found myself speechless.

He took one look at me—he was probably used to the attention—chuckled and held out his hand. I stood up and extended mine to him. Instead of shaking it, he surrounded it by both of his and brought it to his lips. "Good morning, madam. I am Ezra Yoke." He gave me a quick bow. This was certainly a day for bows. Two men had bowed to me in the same day. I wondered what that meant. Was I about to become a princess or something?

"My name is Lorry Lockharte, Mr. Yoke. How can I help you?"

"Oh, Miss Lockharte, please call me Ezra. And may I call you Lorry?"

You wouldn't believe what I did then. I blushed! Like a school girl! "Yes, you may," I sighed, looking up into his eyes like a lovesick puppy.

"Lorry, I used to help out Betty—poor thing. I heard about what happened, falling down the stairs and all.

How tragic. Anyway, I used to help her out upstairs—arranging those files up there. I was wondering—if I might be a help to you and could continue that service?"

My mind was reeling as he talked, and I was thinking that if I said yes, I would get to see him again. And maybe again and again. "Oh, yes," I murmured, "that would be lovely." I almost said enchanting, but he wasn't asking me to go dancing, he was asking me to move some boxes. Saying lovely was bad enough.

He kissed my hand again. I was so engrossed in exploring the depths of his eyes that I didn't even realize he was still holding it. "Thank you, dear Lorry. I'll see you later." Bowing again, Mr. Ezra Yoke, distinguished gentleman that he was, walked to the back and up the stairs.

I sighed. Be still my heart. Then I sneezed.

CHAPTER EIGHTEEN

AFTER MR. EZRA Yoke walked away, and sufficient time had passed for me to regain my senses, I said his name over and over again. Ezra Yoke, Ezra Yoke, Ezra Yoke. Then I moved on. Mrs. Ezra Yoke. Lorry Yoke. Yuck. That made it sound like Lorry Yokel. No problem. I would just keep my own name like I did with Eddie.

I had spent maybe two minutes with the man, and I swear he had me hypnotized. When Mr. Ezra Yoke looked at me, it was like I was the only woman in the entire world—no—the entire universe. That's how completely he gave me his attention. It was the best feeling I could imagine.

Minutes passed and my breathing resumed its normal rhythm. I thought about Mr. Ezra Yoke being upstairs, and then I realized that to get up the stairs, he had to see the body outline on the floor. He had already known about Betty, so he would probably assume it was her. But there were customers coming soon, if I could judge by the phone call. That outline had to go!

I picked up the phone and called the sheriff's station. When they answered, I asked for Sheriff Billy. He was busy interviewing a suspect. So I asked if maybe someone else would know if I could remove the tape on the floor. The woman who answered the phone—I thought it might be the same woman who had taken my fingerprints—said Billy would be back momentarily, but she would go ask. When she returned, she apologized and said it should have been removed already. I thanked her for her time, hung up, and hurried to pull up the tape before anyone else saw it.

It was stickier and more difficult to remove than I thought, but the good part was that it came up clean and left no sticky residue behind. Mr. Ezra Yoke was singing softly to himself upstairs, which made me smile. I was about to look for something to clean off all the fingerprint dust when I heard the bell jingle as the front door opened. A quick glance around told me there was no dust in the exhibit area, so I walked briskly to the front to greet whoever had come in.

It was a family of three. The husband had on a Hawaiian shirt and madras shorts in contrasting colors. The wife wore white capris with a small stain on the pocket, and a pink frilly blouse. They both had on running shoes. The young boy looked ten years old and was clearly more interested in his iPhone than he was in experiencing the historical society.

"Hello!" I gave them a big smile. "Welcome to the Rutledge Historical Society! Can I help you with something, or did you just want to see the exhibits?"

"Hello!" said the husband and wife together. The boy didn't look up from his game. I knew it was a game because I could hear the bells and buzzers. "We'd just like to look at the exhibits."

"Follow me." When I got to the foot of the stairs, I

held out my left arm to show them where to start. They nodded their thank yous, and stepped into the exhibit area—the boy with his head still buried in his iPhone.

I sat down at the desk and glanced into the gift shop which was behind the glass partition by the front door. Neither Martha nor Petra had ever given me instructions on either the gift shop or where she kept the money for change. Standing up and walking up to the glass, I gave it a long look. The gift shop wasn't that big, but there were many items for sale from t-shirts to postcards. Mentally, I went over the money in my purse. I had the money that I had cashed from Martha's check, but it was all in big bills. Besides that, I had maybe one twenty-dollar bill, one five, and a handful of small change. If they bought something and needed change, it might be a problem. If worse came to worst, I could ask them to get change next door at the Koffee Korner.

I turned on the computer. While I waited for it to start up, I turned my chair around and looked at the tropical fish. Watching fish swim was so relaxing. Now that Eddie was out of my life, I could allow myself to enjoy them again. When I was with him, instead of arguing, it was always easier to go along with everything he wanted. He always got his way, anyway. So now, I could enjoy the fish.

There were wiggly Black Moors, black and orange Oranda goldfish, and some Calico Fantails. They were beautiful, and it was so pleasant to watch them. If it hadn't been for my fish tank when I was in high school, I might not have made it through. I could get lost in watching those fish.

My peace was interrupted when I noticed the computer had finished starting up. Turning around to try out my email, I clicked on the email program, and Betty's email was still there. Well, I didn't have to delete it to get to my own. I knew a thing or two about computers, so I clicked on settings and set up my email account. A minute later, one message downloaded. It was from Petra, and the subject was *Did You Start Your Divorce Yet?* There was nothing else to the message. Before I could reply the family walked into the gift shop. I kept my fingers crossed.

They walked out a few minutes later with three postcards and handed them to me. One was a front picture of the Coyote Moon Casino; the second was a picture of the river when it was really rushing, which hadn't been for years, maybe decades; and the third was a picture of the original front of the Rutledge Historical Society building before the bright yellow Rutledge Koffee Korner Kafe had changed it to a hysterical building. They paid seventy-five cents in cash. When they left, I put the three quarters on Petra's desk.

Then I noticed Rocky the cat curled up on Petra's chair. "You, *thing*! Get out of here!" Its eyes slowly opened, it stretched, and then instead of jumping down and going someplace else like I wanted it to, it ignored me and lay down again and went back to sleep. I sneezed and rubbed my itchy nose.

CHAPTER NINETEEN

AS I WAS about to return to the back room to clean up the fingerprint dust, my email program beeped. I was beginning to think I was better off without it. Clicking the email, I saw it was from Martha. She would be sending a courier over with some paperwork to type. If I had any questions, call her. She gave me her number.

Which reminded me. The blotter on the desk still said April, and it had been May for a week already. I ripped the dirty sheet off, copied Martha's number onto May, and folded the old one up. I would check with Petra in case there was something on there that she needed.

Then the bell jingled and the door opened. A fifteen-year-old boy stood there with an envelope in his hand. I knew he was fifteen because his t-shirt said *I just turned fifteen and all I got for my birthday was this lousy t-shirt*. It looked new. He handed me the envelope, and I thanked him. He rode off on a bicycle. I wondered why he wasn't in school.

Opening the envelope, I found five documents. Three that were one page each, one that was three pages, and the final one which was five pages. They all needed editing. It would probably take me the rest of the afternoon. There went my chance to clean up the fingerprint dust and look around back there.

I had just finished the third document when the bell jingled and the door opened producing Eddie. I glanced at him and his seductive smile, and I decided to ignore him. So I kept typing. My chair was in a position so I could see him reflected in the computer screen.

"Truck? Remember what was going to happen today? You were going to give me some money." He put out his hand palm up. "Come on now. Give it up like a good girl."

"Go away, Eddie. I'm not buying what you're selling. Leave me alone."

While I was facing the computer screen, he stepped closer and picked something up off the desk. My purse was in the drawer, so I knew it wasn't that.

"What's this? I hope it's somebody else's, because there's no way I'll give you a divorce!"

I turned around with a smile on my face. "Irreconcilable differences, buddy boy. I don't need *you* to sign *anything*! Now go back to the hole you crawled out of." Turning around to the computer, I added, "It's too bad that I can't enumerate to the court all your many infidelities and how much money of *ours* that you lost."

He put his hand on my shoulder and roughly pulled me around so I was facing him. It shocked me. He had never hit me before or behaved in any kind of physically abusive manner. Eddie did have his good points. Now that I was facing him, I held up my forefinger and pointed it at him. "Leave me alone and get out of here! I mean now!"

"You *owe* me, Lorry! You better get some money

together and—"

He didn't get to finish his sentence. In the heat of our argument, Mr. Ezra Yoke had come down the stairs unnoticed by either of us. Now he stood between us, towering over Eddie. "Is this gentleman bothering you, Lorry?"

It was obvious to both Eddie and me that a man dressed in an expensive suit like Ezra had on would not fight with him. What was strange is that we had no idea what he *might* do, and although there was no threatening tone in what Ezra had said, there was something foreboding about the way he had said it.

Eddie turned around and opened the door before I had a chance to speak. "I'll be back, Lorry," he said without an accent, then he closed the door. He had dropped the divorce papers on the floor as he left.

Ezra stepped forward, opened the door, and called after Eddie, "And I'll be here!" Then he closed the door.

I took a deep breath and tried to relax. Ezra took a step toward my desk, grabbed my hand, and pulled me up out of my seat. "I think you need a hug, Lorry." This girl wasn't going to argue. If a hunk of a man like that wanted to hug me, it was okay with me. And he was a really good hugger. When he stopped and stepped back, I was disappointed. It had been a long time since I had a hug like that.

"Are you going to be okay?"

"Yes, I'll be fine. Thank you, Ezra. I don't know what got into Eddie. He's never acted like that before. He's always been a jerk—but he's never threatened me like that."

Ezra bent down, picked up the divorce papers, glanced at them, straightened them on the desk, and handed them to me. "This must have been why he was angry. He doesn't want to lose you. Can't say that I blame him."

I took the papers and blushed. This man really got to me! "Thank you, Ezra."

"I'll see you in a day or two to get some more work done. Goodbye, Lorry. I hope the jerk leaves you alone." He opened the door and disappeared out of it before I even had a chance to say goodbye.

Taking another deep breath, I turned around to face the fish tank again. At that moment, I needed the gentle motions of the fish to calm me. A few minutes later, I had already become lost in their smooth movements, and I felt better. As I was trying to refocus on the document I had been typing, the bell jingled and the door opened again. It was a courier—not the fifteen-year-old boy this time. It was a professional courier company.

The man in the uniform stepped in. "A package for Lorry Lockharte." He had a large envelope in his hand.

"That's me. I'm Lorry Lockharte." I stood up and reached for it.

"I'm sorry, ma'am. Do you have identification?"

After I fished my driver's license out of my purse and showed it to him, he released the envelope to me. What was this? I wasn't expecting anything. Almost no one knew I even worked here. There was a business envelope inside. It was from McGowan and Wake Attorneys at Law. My mother's lawyers. I ripped open the envelope and unfolded the letter. A check for five hundred dollars fell out. The letter said the money was to be used to facilitate the divorce from Mr. Edward Keeley. How did they even know? And more than that, they had told me previously that since my mother had disinherited me, all her money had been given to charity when she died. So where did the five hundred dollars come from?

CHAPTER TWENTY

AS I WORKED on the final two documents, my mind raced as I typed. It was a curious phenomenon: If I could put my mind someplace else as I typed, I found that I could type much faster than if I focused on each word. Once I finished editing the documents, I could fly over them as long as I thought of something else. So my mind centered on the letter and check from my mother's attorneys. How could they possibly know that I was thinking of divorcing Eddie?

Wait! Cancel that thought! I wasn't *thinking* of divorcing Eddie, I was *definitely* going to divorce Eddie. This check represented some kind of sign that I was moving in the right direction. Judging from Eddie's recent visit, maybe I didn't even need a sign. I had put up with a lot of insults and humiliations over the years, but he had never been physical with me before. With today's visit so fresh on my mind, it made me wonder if this was a new Eddie. A new and more dangerous Eddie.

He had abused me both mentally and emotionally numerous times, forcing me to do things I didn't want to do—like giving up Bingo—and to force me into a mold that *he* thought I should be. And I allowed all of it. But I wouldn't accept or allow physical abuse. Maybe I didn't need the sign. Maybe I was starting to be a new and stronger me. At that moment I realized that today was the first day of the rest of my life. A cliché, yes, but that's how I felt. And that life did not include Eddie.

That brought me back to thoughts of the check. How could they know the exact day that I had received the forms to fill out? The first day I had actually considered it and taken getting a divorce seriously. My fingers stopped typing in the middle of a word. Immediately, I was livid! There was only one way they could have known, and that would be kaleidoscope girl! How dare she butt her nose into my business. How dare she take it upon herself to contact the lawyers and report on me like a little spy. I appreciate that she printed out the divorce forms for me, but this was too much, and I wouldn't stand for it.

It took me a few minutes to calm myself enough to continue typing. And I wouldn't allow myself to think of Petra and her tattletaling on me—even though it benefited me. When I finished the documents, I attached them to an email and sent them along to Martha. Then I leafed through the forms that kaleidoscope girl had printed for me. Thinking of her name would just rev me up again.

The first form I had to fill out was titled Petition for Dissolution of Marriage. I decided they spelled it wrong. It should be Disillusion of Marriage. The beginning questions were easy: my name and address, occupation, and how long I've lived in Arizona. Then, same questions about Eddie. What should I put for his occupation? Oh, that was an easy one. Gambler. Losing gambler would be more accurate. And filling out the paperwork made me realize something else: I needed to get a permanent address. Since I didn't know how long I would be at Martha's, I didn't want to use her address. I'd have to get a post office box first chance I got.

When I was halfway through the first form, Kasey came in. "Hi, Lorry. Sorry I've been too busy to stop by. I—" She stopped in mid-sentence, which was unusually rare for her. Usually she didn't stop talking until someone else butted their way in. "You're filling out divorce forms! You're divorcing Eddie! Whoopee! Congratulations!" She clapped her hands and jumped up and down. Sometimes her enthusiasm annoyed me. No, that's not right. It *always* annoyed me.

She walked out the door. It had barely closed when she stuck her head back in. "By the way, Lorry, several people from school have come in, and I told all of them that you were back in town and worked here now. So don't be surprised if anyone drops by to see you! Bye!"

And she was gone. By school, she meant high school. Kasey never went to college. She had gotten married out of high school and gone straight to work. She didn't have a kid until years later, so it wasn't one of those forced marriages.

That was one thing I had to thank Eddie for—my completing college—even though he had ulterior motives, which of course I didn't realize at the time. Whenever I suggested that I wanted to quit college, he always talked me out of it. Why? The reason had escaped me back then, but the whole time I was in college, my mother gave me an allowance. A generous allowance. An allowance that allowed me and Eddie to live quite comfortably. As long as I kept a B average or better, the checks kept coming.

When I graduated, Eddie tried to talk me into continuing school, but I had no interest. There was a disconcerting time for us after that, when I didn't know whether Eddie would leave me or not. I didn't realize at the time why he was even considering it, because we were getting along fine then. Finally, though, he decided to stay. Now I realize how blessed I would have been had he left. That realization was a long time coming. What hit me as strange at the time was that he went from thinking about leaving me to asking me to marry him. Only now can I understand the implications of that. He was hoping for my mother's money.

I had completed most of the forms when Petra came in. She had a huge smile on her face. I was going to wipe that grin off her face and enjoy doing it. She had no business poking her nose into my private affairs—even if she *was* the one who printed up the forms for me.

CHAPTER TWENTY-ONE

"HI, LORRY!" SHE smiled at me. She was wearing a ruffled blouse and a blue skirt to match. The skirt was so short that if she raised her hand, you could see places where the sun doesn't even think about shining.

"Petra!" I said, before she reached her office.

She stopped short and looked at me. "Lorry, what's wrong? Why are you looking at me like that?"

"Petra, you had no business telling anyone I was planning to divorce Eddie. Especially—"

"*What* are you talking about? I haven't said a word to anyone!" She sounded sincere, but I knew a lie when I heard it.

"Then who told my mother's lawyers I was getting a divorce? Tell me that, then!" I was furious, and I was screaming.

"I have no idea what you're talking about. How would *I* know who your mother's lawyers are?" She didn't yell back. She answered me in her normal voice.

"You know perfectly well—" I stopped. How *would* she know who my mother's lawyers were? Maybe I didn't know a lie when I heard one.

"Tell me what happened," said Petra.

"Now I'm more confused than ever. If *you* didn't tell the lawyers, then who did?" I handed her the letter.

Petra read it over quickly. "They enclosed a check for five hundred dollars?" I held up the check and waved it. She read the letter again and then picked the envelope up off my desk. "Lorry, I don't get it. How would they know? When did you start thinking about divorcing Eddie? It was just today, wasn't it?"

"That's not quite correct. I've been thinking about a divorce for ten years, but have only just now been serious about it." It was true. Every time I caught him being unfaithful, which was often, and every time he lost a bunch of *my* money, which was often, I thought about divorcing him. But he always sweet-talked me into staying. And fool that I was, I stayed.

"What are you going to do now?"

I smiled for the first time then. "I'm going to get me a divorce!" I held up my hand, and she high-fived me. "I'm sorry I accused you of that, Petra. Really. I apologize."

She shrugged. "Do you need any help with the forms?"

"No. I need to get a post office box, so I can have a proper address."

"You can use this address. Martha would be fine with that."

Shaking my head, I said, "I don't think that's such a good idea. It would be better if I had my own real address. I haven't taken a lunch since I started working here, but do you think it would be all right if I closed for ten minutes so I could run over to the post office?"

"Oh, sure! You can close for an hour. Betty used to do

that all the time."

She opened the second drawer of my desk and pulled out a small sign that had a clock with movable hands and the words *Be Right Back!* The first time I looked in the drawer I didn't notice it because the sign had been face down.

"You can use this, Lorry. No problem. But if you want to go now, it would be fine, too."

"No, I think I'd rather finish these forms. Now that I have the money, I'm eager to get the thing started."

I considered telling her about Mr. Ezra Yoke saving me from Eddie earlier that day, but I didn't know what kind of reflection on Ezra it might be, so I decided not to. It would be a horrible reflection on Eddie, but she already thought the worst of him, so I didn't need to make him out as more of a bad guy than he already was.

As she started walking back to her office, I called her back. "Hey, Petra. You looked really happy when you came in. What's the big smile about?"

"Oh!" Her face lit up again. "My boyfriend is coming to town!"

"Petra, that's awesome!" I said trying to sound enthusiastic. Maybe I needed to take lessons from Kasey. Petra's boyfriend was probably some tattooed-up biker.

When she walked out of the room again, I thought of something else. "Petra?"

"Yeah?" she asked from her office.

"Come back a sec."

"Yeah?"

Leaning forward in my chair, I said in a loud whisper, "If *you* didn't tell the lawyers, then how did they know?"

"Lorry, I have no idea. Really."

I looked around the office, at my desk, the computer,

the picture on the wall, and finally my eyes rested on the fish tank. I watched the fish for a few seconds as if a camera might be hidden behind the googley eyes of a Black Moor. "No." Shaking my head, I looked at Petra again. "Do you think someone is watching me?"

Petra had a funny expression on her face—a sympathetic fake smile. "What else could it be, Lorry?"

Her response made me shiver. I looked around again and saw someone approaching the door. The bell announced the door opening. It was Michael Wellesley. Instead of a suit, he wore brand new unwashed blue jeans and a white shirt with a pastel green sweater vest over it.

He nodded to me and looked at Petra. "Martha had asked me to let you know when the funeral would be. It's Saturday at Rutledge Cemetery. Eleven o'clock."

"I'm really sorry, Michael," said Petra.

He looked down and shook his head slowly. "I came to arrange one funeral and ended up arranging two. It had been so long since I had seen my sisters. I feel so guilty about that." He looked up then. "It's not like we didn't communicate—we weren't estranged or anything. But it was only Christmas or birthdays. We had lost touch over the years. I guess that's my fault, I should have made more of an effort."

Petra came over and put her hand on his arm. "It's all right, Michael. I'm sure they understood that you were busy with your own life."

Michael nodded. "Then I think if I had only arrived in town earlier, I might have been able to prevent it."

Petra shrugged. "When did you get here?"

"Yesterday morning." His eyes drifted to the right, then looked down again, out the window by my desk, and then back at her. "Well, I better get going now. Goodbye."

Petra and I both said goodbye to him. We watched him through the window walk down the street. As soon as he was out of sight, Petra said, "He's lying."

CHAPTER TWENTY-TWO

"WAIT. WHAT?" I asked, shocked.

"He's lying through his teeth."

"How could you possibly know that? The man is distraught."

"That may or may not be true. But he's lying. And this is how I know. I studied it. When you ask a person a question, if their gaze goes to the left, then they're trying to remember the answer. For instance, if I asked you when was the last time you saw an Alaska license plate, your gaze would wander left as you tried to remember. But if your gaze goes to the right, you're telling a lie. When I asked him when he got to town, he looked to the right when he answered. That means he was here before yesterday morning."

My gaze wandered to the left as I put it together. "Which means he was here in time to do the killing."

Petra's eyes went up, and she nodded. "Yup."

"But was he here when Betty died?"

"What difference does it make?" Petra asked.

"Because I don't think that was an accident. And that would make all the difference. Which reminds me—tell me about Zackary James."

Petra turned away. "What's to tell?"

"Petra, come on. Be honest with me. I saw you go pale when Billy mentioned his name. What's that about?"

She shook her head, but when I pressed her to tell me, she said, "Okay! Zack and I have known each other since grade school. He lived down the block from me. But the reason we were close is because our fathers used to take us to the same bars. We played together. In the bars. It was sick, and we were kind of each other's savior in that way."

"So, were you involved with him?"

"Oh, no. It was never like that. We were best friends. We both knew *exactly* what the other was going through." She took a couple of steps back into the room and leaned against the door. "When we got to high school, I buried myself in my studies got good grades. Zack kept getting into trouble. Part of it was that his father used to beat him and his mother."

"Wow." I couldn't think of anything more profound to say.

She suddenly looked up and said forcefully, "But he would *never* hurt anyone. *Never*. That's just not like Zack. He got caught the first time because someone came home and found him there stealing stuff. He could have run. It was an older couple. Instead of even *pushing them over*, he gave himself up." She shook her head. "He's a gentle soul, Lorry. He would never hurt anyone."

I nodded. "I believe you, Petra."

Her voice got softer. "And the reason his prints were on the back door is because he was probably coming to see me. He tried the back because he didn't want anyone to see him here."

"You need to talk to Billy. You know, like a character witness."

She shook her head. "I can't get involved. It might hurt my chances with college."

"What do you mean you can't get involved? To save your friend? Besides, I thought it was a done deal already."

"Not until I begin classes in the summer. And they can kick me out anytime for a number of different reasons. I can't do it."

"Then I'll do it! I'll call Billy right now!" I reached for the phone.

"Really? You'd do that for a guy you don't even know?"

"It's about justice, Petra. If he's innocent, then someone needs to defend him. If you won't, I will." I paused with the phone in my hand and looked at her with what I hoped was my hard gaze. "Of course, it would go a lot farther if it wasn't just hearsay—if he heard it from someone who really knew him."

"Have him come over here. I'll stay in my office and see how it goes. If it looks like you need help"—she shook her head—"I'll try to do it in a way that won't get me involved."

"I don't understand, Petra. Billy is your friend. He loaned you that money. Can't you ask him not to involve you?"

"You don't understand, Lorry. What's between me and Billy has nothing to do with his job as sheriff. If I ask him not to involve me, that goes beyond our friendship. I can't do it."

"I'll call him now, and we'll see how it goes."

Sheriff Billy reluctantly agreed to stop by. He was in

the office a grand total of three minutes. I laid it all out for him, said that Petra would verify what I said if he needed her to, and his answer was not no, but absolutely no. Zackary was his main and only suspect, and unless I could give Billy a lot more compelling evidence than "But he's a nice guy," then Zackary would stay incarcerated and still be the suspect. When I reminded him that I thought Betty's death wasn't an accident and that Zack wasn't yet released when that death had happened, he told me to prove that it wasn't an accident. He said *that* would be compelling evidence.

After he left, Petra and I looked at each other and shook our heads. What had to happen next was perfectly clear. I had to prove that Betty's death was no accident.

CHAPTER TWENTY-THREE

IT WAS THE end of another thought-provoking day, and I was ready to go home. Or at least to Martha's B&B, which was as close to home as I could get these days. As I walked past Petra's desk, she was engrossed in Quickbooks, with Rocky the cat on her lap. I could hear him purring from across the room. Every once in a while, between keystrokes, Petra would take one hand off the keyboard and pet him. Why anyone would want to do that was beyond me. I sneezed.

"Gesundheit! You leaving, Lorry?" She didn't turn around, just kept stroking the cat.

"Yup. I'll see you tomorrow."

"Remember, go to lunch tomorrow and just put that sign up. It will be fine."

"All right, thanks. Goodbye, Petra!"

"Bye!"

I walked through the back, stepping over the one box and alongside the others. It reminded me that I still hadn't gone through the rest of the exhibits. Although I thought that maybe I should do it the following day, I wanted to work on Betty's non-accidental death. It didn't add up to me, and I couldn't let it go.

My car started right up, so I patted the dashboard in approval. Then I drove straight home to Martha's house. This time I parked in front, walked up to the door, and knocked.

Martha answered the door this time, not wearing jeans and not wearing what she had when I saw her earlier. It was a pale pink suit with pink heels to match. For her age, she looked beautiful. No, she looked beautiful, regardless. "Lorry! I forgot to give you a key yesterday! No need to be knocking on the door all the time!" She turned around to the antique side table by the front door, picked up a key, and handed it to me. "And listen, Hugo and I are going out, but he made a little something for lunch. There's plenty left over, and you're welcome to have it. And of course you can use our kitchen any time, but as long as we cook dinner most nights, how about I charge you an extra five dollars and you eat with us? Does that sound all right?"

I nodded with what must have been a look on my face that was halfway between gratitude and dumb luck. But it reminded me that I hadn't paid her yet. "Oh! That reminds me." I dug into my purse and handed her the money from the check I had cashed that morning. "Here's the money for rent. Let me know when I owe you more."

She took the money and looked at it without counting. "This should last awhile." Hugo came down the stairs at that moment wearing a suit and tie and looking rather dashing. "Time for us to leave! Bye, Lorry!" Martha held out the door, and Hugo walked through smiling at me.

"Hi, Lorry! Bye, Lorry!" he said.

"Bye, Hugo!"

I stood there, alone in the house. Since I didn't have a chance to look around the day before when I arrived, I thought I might as well use this opportunity. The tall table by the door was the only furniture in the entryway. It was roundish, with beveled edges, on a pedestal base with three curved legs. The top of the table had an inlay in a darker wood that followed the shape of the table. In the center of the table was a painted picture of a rose. Just beneath the top of the table was a "skirt" that followed the bevels of the top. It was carved with roses that matched the top. The curved legs of the table had the same inlaid darker wood on the edges.

Turning toward my right, I peered into the living room. There was a fireplace on one side with a couch, a love seat, and a matching chair surrounding it. An oval table with a marble top sat in the middle of the grouping. Its legs followed the same curves as the table in the entryway. The couch was of a chintz fabric in uneven blue stripes, and the back of the couch had a wooden ornamentation on it that almost looked like a crown.

The room was a pale beige, but the base molding on the floor and the wood surrounding the fireplace was white. On the top of the mantel were several pictures of children along with a menorah in the center. I knew what a menorah was because of my friend Sam. It was one of those candelabra used by Jewish families for Hanukah and who knows what else.

On the other side of the room, installed bookcases lined the wall. Three bookcases that surrounded the window and were filled with mostly paperback books had a small sign on them that said "Take one, leave one." Opposite the window was another couch, love seat, and a chair set that was antique but didn't look as old or in as good condition as the main one. It was a darker beige than the walls and had dark wood trim with matching legs. The fabric was a deep plush and looked more comfortable and inviting than the other couch set.

Everything was beautiful and in pristine condition. I turned around and stepped into the dining room. The table was not antique, but had plenty of room for B&B guests to sit at. Behind it was a beautiful glassed-in hutch displaying what looked like fine china.

The whole house reminded me so much of the house I grew up in that it made me sad. Then I remembered the five hundred dollar check in my pocket. My mother didn't abandon me after all. There was a certain amount of satisfaction in that thought. And then my phone rang and ruined the little amount of joy that I derived from that thought. It was Eddie.

CHAPTER TWENTY-FOUR

I DIDN'T ANSWER the phone when Eddie called. After running up the stairs two at a time—which wasn't easy considering I still had my heels on, but I did hold onto the rail—I sat in the chair in my bedroom and read the time-travel romance novel I had bought when I was staying at the motel. The characters could come and go from the nineteenth century to the twenty-first century through a cave. It was pretty cool. And the men in it were hot! Be still my heart.

Eddie had left a message. I decided that I wouldn't even listen to it until morning. But at three A.M. I was wide awake wondering what he said. So, in an effort not to wake Martha and Hugo, I pulled the phone under the covers and muffled it with blankets before I listened to it. Too many blankets. I couldn't hear a thing, so I had to play it again.

"Lorry!" he said, in a tone that made it sound like it was all right to talk to me like that, "I need the money. I realize that you're not really going to divorce me— because you never do—but still, I have to tell you that it hurt seeing those papers on your desk. To make it up to me, why don't you take me to dinner tomorrow? I'll pay the tip. Then you can give me more money, too. I know you have some. So how about it? Let me know. If I don't hear from you, I'll stop by tomorrow. That old guy in the suit didn't scare me. I'll see you tomorrow."

For some reason, I didn't delete it. I suppose I wanted to torture myself with it again. How dare he call Ezra an old guy. He wasn't old, he was mature and sophisticated. Eddie never did have any taste. Wait a minute—I think I just insulted myself. After I put the phone away, it took a long time to go back to sleep. What I came up with, after turning from one side to the other, was that I had to file for divorce before I lost my nerve, or I broke down and gave Eddie the money. No! I wouldn't do that! Would I? Shaking my head, I fell asleep with tears in my eyes. Because I had done that more times than I could count.

The following morning at breakfast, I asked Martha if it was okay to come in a little late so I could file for divorce. Her response surprised me.

"Yes, that would be fine. I did hear that your ex-husband had been coming in and harassing you." She took another bite of toast. "Just make sure that Petra is in this morning before you go."

It really was a small town. Now that I was back and away from the hustle and bustle of Coyote Moon, I was starting to like being back. It felt comfortable having everyone know my business. It felt familiar. And it didn't feel bad at all. I knew some people hated that aspect of small-town living, but for me, I honestly liked it. Because it made me feel safe and secure. At that moment, I must have forgotten that one person was murdered—and very likely two people—at the place where I worked. Still, small towns felt safer than the anonymity of the big city

108

—or even the small city.

When I drove by the front of the historical society, Petra was just walking in. I called her over to my car. "Petra! Come here!"

She walked to the curb and smiled at me. "Good morning, Lorry."

"Will you be here so I can file for divorce this morning? Martha said it was okay as long as you were here."

"Sure. I have to leave by nine o'clock."

"I'll be back by then."

"If you get hung up, it's okay. I'll put out the sign that you'll be back in fifteen minutes. That will give you an extra half hour." She laughed. "People always figure those signs are wrong. Good luck!" She waved and walked into the building, turned the light on, and put the *Open* sign out.

CHAPTER TWENTY-FIVE

MY FIRST STOP was the post office to get an address to write on the forms. That reminded me that I didn't have Eddie's address, and there was no way I was going to ask him for it. I'd find out soon enough if that was a problem.

I drove part way down the street and pulled into the lot behind the post office. As soon as I got inside, I saw there was a line just to get the form for the post office box. Checking my watch, I frowned. It would take longer than I had expected. When I got to the front of the line, the clerk said I had to fill out the papers elsewhere. I asked if I could come to the front of the line when I finished, and he shrugged his shoulders and said, "Sorry."

I filled the whole form out except where it wanted my physical address. Stepping outside to see the address of the historical society, I squinted and saw 852 Main Street. By the time I got back in line, the line had grown. It took ten more minutes to get back to the window and pay for the box. I only rented for six months. Hopefully before then I would have my own place again. At least my own rental. My watch said eight forty-five. I didn't want Petra to put up that sign, so I'd have to start the divorce papers at lunch. But I had time to stop at the bank real quick and cash the check my mother had sent me.

I knew that *she* didn't really send it to me. It was so unexpected, though, that it *felt* like she had sent it, and I appreciated that. After cashing the check, I arrived at the historical society at five minutes before nine. Petra was at the front door when I walked in. "Hey! You're ducking out five minutes early! No fair!"

She looked up and pulled the *Be Right Back!* sign off the door. "Chill, will ya? I was just putting the sign on the door." She walked back to her desk, and the cat was on her chair looking up at her and meowing. "Oh, no! I forgot to feed Rocky, and now I'm going to be late. Can you feed him for me, Lorry? Please? His food and his dish are in the cabinet in the bathroom. When he's finished eating, be sure to wash his dish. Martha doesn't want it to attract rodents." Next thing I knew, she was out the door.

First, I put my purse in the bottom desk drawer and started to walk back to the cat, when I thought twice about it. Stepping back across the room, I took the purse out of the drawer and brought it with me to the bathroom. Eddie had never come to see me in the morning, but I didn't want to take any chances. Usually in the mornings, he would be in the Coyote Moon poker room trying to get in a game where the people were too tired to realize how bad they were losing. When I wasn't working, I'd go with him and feel bored out of my mind while he thoroughly enjoyed himself losing *my* money.

Rocky the cat followed me into the bathroom. When I

opened the cabinet, as I stuck my hand in to grab his dish, I sneezed, which sent poor Rocky reeling backward. If I had any affection for cats, I would have laughed. Oh, wait. I did laugh. Pulling out the cat dish and a package of kibble, I poured some in. I had no idea how much to feed him. He was rubbing himself against my legs, and he looked chubby. So I poured some back into the package and then set the dish down next to the water. When I saw that water the other day, I should have known what it might mean. I sneezed. It meant allergies. Yuck. I sneezed again and rubbed my nose.

Back at my desk, I stuck the purse back into the drawer and turned on the computer. Oops. I had forgotten to turn it off the previous day. I'd have to talk to Petra to see if I messed up anything. There was no email, so I took the old blotter page out of my desk where I had stashed it and brought it over to Petra's desk. Then I wrote a note on it: *Do you need this for anything or can I toss it? Lorry*.

The cat jumped up on the chair and meowed in my face. "If that's thank you, Rocky, you're welcome. Now leave me alone." He meowed again. "Not enough food for you today? Tough. You're on a diet, just like I should be. Go upstairs now or wherever you hang out these days. Bye!" I would have given him a little pat on the behind to get him going, but I didn't want to touch him and risk breaking out in hives. Instead, I walked to the back room, washed his food dish, put it away, and gave him fresh water. While I was in the service cabinet, I spied a dust cloth and took it out along with a can of Dust 'N Clean. Yes! Good reminder. Now I could get rid of the fingerprint dust.

CHAPTER TWENTY-SIX

WHEN I RETURNED to my office, I realized I had left my purse in the drawer. Luckily, neither Eddie nor anyone else had come in while I was in the back looking after the cat. I opened the drawer, took out a tissue from my purse, blew my nose, and checked my email again. Still nothing. The bottom drawer had a lock mechanism on it, and I thought how ideal it would be if I could lock the drawer and not have to worry about Eddie coming in and stealing my money. It was an old desk, but there was always a chance. So I stuck my hand inside the top drawer moving around the pens, pencils, paper clips, staples, and whatnot that was in there. In the back corner under some papers I didn't bother to look at, I found a key.

First, I took out my purse. I didn't want to take a chance of locking the drawer, not being able to unlock it, and having my purse stuck inside. Then I tried the key. It went in easily and turned. As I tugged on the drawer, I saw that it was locked firmly. I reinserted the key and opened the drawer. Then I put my purse inside the drawer and relocked it. What to do with the key so no one would find it? Reaching into the back of the drawer underneath the same papers where I had found it, I replaced the key.

Standing up, I was getting ready to go into the back to start cleaning when I saw four people walk by the window and turn toward the historical society's door. The bell jingled, and four people from my high school walked in. Jason Compton, Thomas Patterson, Ashley McEnroe, and Renee Croft.

Jason, wearing light gray jeans and a dark gray sweater, had been captain of the football team. He had always been good looking—still was—and I had a crush on him at one time, but so did most girls in the school. He had never paid me any attention. Although I heard at one time he had dabbled in real estate for a while—unsuccessfully—now he was enjoying the lifestyle of the rich and famous. Or just rich. His family was filthy rich, and I do mean filthy. His father had made his money using cheap labor in Asia and selling at high prices.

Thomas Patterson wore slacks and an Izod shirt. He was a linebacker on the football team, mean and brutish on the field and sweet as a lamb off. His family didn't have money, and I could never understand how he had wormed his way into the group. Must be blackmail or something. He had tried to get into the police force but failed the physical exam because of an old football injury. Last I heard he was doing security at a factory in Coyote Moon but still living here in Rutledge.

The two men both had blond hair and blue eyes. They could have been surfers if Arizona wasn't landlocked. Jason was tall and thin, and Tom was hefty and solid.

Ashley McEnroe's family had more money than the queen. She wore a short skirt with an expensive designer blouse. She was dark-haired and dark-eyed. Ashley had never worked and never would. No one knew how her father had made his money, but everyone respected him. She had never acted rude toward me and was usually the one who said hello in the halls—sometimes even if she was with someone else.

Renee Croft was my nemesis. She had blond hair and blue eyes and had what Eddie liked to call an "hourglass figure." We went to the same college briefly, and she always made fun of me for dating Eddie. Personally, I think she wanted him for herself. Heaven only knew why.

But she would always remind me of my sister's death. Renee was in the car the night my sister died. Two people died, two lived. The other person who lived didn't come out as lucky as Renee; he had lived ever since in a convalescent home due to his severe injuries. Rumor had it—and I believed it—that although Renee reported that the boy killed was the one driving, it had actually been her. She and the dead boy were the only ones out of the car when the cops came. The boy, already deceased, was half in and half out of the driver's seat with the door open. Renee was climbing out of the back seat—or trying to—because there wasn't much left of the back seat.

Alcohol had been involved, but since Renee "wasn't driving," no charges were filed. It was too convenient that the boy killed was supposedly driving. The other boy —the one currently in the convalescent home—had brain injuries and couldn't remember anything, including who had been driving. My sister, Lauren, and the boy she was dating were both already gone when the ambulance arrived. The strange thing is that Lauren and her boyfriend had started the evening seated together in the back seat. Why had the girls ended up together in the back? And why was Lauren's boyfriend driving when it was the other guy's car? It didn't make sense. But it wasn't enough to provoke an investigation, and Renee stuck to her story.

There was no question that she was strong enough to move the boy into the driver's seat. She was a gymnast, tall and strong. Renee was probably strong enough to pick up the whole car.

These people were not my friends. They had *never* been my friends, although they were all in the same year I was in. They were in one of the cliques in my high school that never included me or any of my friends. Well, I shouldn't say never. Since I did live in the expensive part of town, they had invited me to join their little group. When they discovered that I refused to act arrogant to everyone else, I was summarily kicked out. After that, except for Ashley, if they ever said hello in the halls, it would only be when nobody else was around to see them condescend to acknowledge me. And yet, here they were in all their glory.

"Hi, Lorry!" They all said nearly in unison. Ashley and Renee gave me a token hug, and the boys stood there looking like boys.

"We heard you were back in town," said Ashley.

"You're working *here* now?" asked Renee, looking around. "Why? It's a total dump."

It wasn't a dump; it was old and historic. And I rather liked it—even if it was the only job I could find. Instead of making an excuse, I decided to play it differently. You know, take the offensive. "I like history. But I remember, Renee, you don't like history much, do you? I remember you didn't do too well in that class."

116

She gave me a dirty look and then looked me up and down. I could tell that she wanted to comment on my clothing, but there was nothing she could say. No matter how broke Eddie and I were, after paying the mortgage and other bills, the first thing I did was shop at Neiman Marcus and Nordstrom's. Nobody could say that I didn't dress well. And today, with my red skirt, just below the knee, red and black striped sweater, and red heels compared to her second-rate slack suit, she wouldn't dare say a word. But then she noticed the dust cloth and can of Dust 'N Clean on the desk.

"So you do the cleaning here as well?" She nodded toward the dust cloth and smiled. "Yes, I suppose that suits you. Perfectly." A rattlesnake would have to slither awfully fast to have venom that potent.

Ashley ignored Renee's comment and looked around. "Yes, I can see this place would have some potential. But those fish would have to go!"

Before I could tell her how much the fish added to the ambiance of the place, Renee came back in for the attack. "So, I heard Eddie dumped you. Again."

"Dumped me?" I smiled at her sweetly. "If you can call *me* leaving *him* in the Grand Canyon without a way home being dumped, then yes, I guess he did. But I enjoyed a pleasant drive home by myself without his incessant whining."

Jason and Tom, thinking they were about to see a cat fight, shuffled uncomfortably. They were either eager to place bets on who would win, or they didn't like being around that kind of haughtiness. Although, since they had been hanging around with Renee for all these years, my guess was they wanted to place bets.

"Well, nice seeing you again, Lorry! We'd better be off

now," said Ashley. She was always fairly pleasant, and I never understood her attraction to that group.

"Yes," said Renee, "we're going to the casino and spend ungodly amounts of money"—she took a step toward me and stopped an inch from my face—"that you unfortunately no longer have! Ha!" Then she turned and strolled out the door, with the others following behind.

CHAPTER TWENTY-SEVEN

WHEN THEY LEFT, I watched as they walked next door to the Koffee Korner Kafe. Then I noticed it. The red mustang that Eddie had driven off in the other day. Where was he? Was he in the Koffee Korner waiting until no one was in here with me? I checked to make sure the drawer with my purse in it was locked, although I already knew that it was. With Eddie, it doesn't hurt to double check. I even gave it a sharp jerk to make sure the lock wasn't some flimsy thing for show. It didn't budge. These old desks were better made than today's cheaper versions.

After making sure there was nothing incriminating on my desk and nothing Eddie could use against me, I hurried to the back room with the dust cloth and can of Dust 'N Clean to start cleaning—and investigating. First task was to go to the back door to get the dust off both handles. The forensic *boys* had wiped some of it off, but I could still feel it on my hands whenever I went in or out the door. Both handles leading to and from the Koffee Korner were dusty, too, so I wiped the one on our side, tried the handle, found it unlocked, and then wiped down the one on their side.

Returning to the area where the box of books was and where I had found poor Gwen's body, I looked for all the places where they had dusted. Since the box of books had been involved with Betty's body and not Gwen's, they hadn't touched it. What else was there? The bottom of the stair railing, the edge of the bookcase, in front of some of the books, and the light switch had all been dusted. I cleaned it all and didn't find much else to clean. So I returned the dust cloth and spray to the bathroom cabinet and came back to look around.

The chain that said *No Admittance* was hooked to the wall divider of the exhibit on one side and to a bookcase on the other. Bookcases filled that whole wall, from the floor almost all the way to the ceiling. At a quick glance, it looked like the books were both fiction and nonfiction on Arizona in general and Rutledge in particular. Although there were books on all the shelves, none of the shelves was full.

On one side of the books, the edge of the bookcase held the books up, and on the other side was a fat, heavy piece of quartz. Some of them were rose quartz; I liked those. I picked two of them up and admired their color and shape. As I started to return one to the shelf, I pulled it back toward me and held it out in front of me. Then I hefted it over my head and brought it down fast. I almost dropped it on the spot. These were heavy enough and big enough to cause damage if you hit someone on the head. They were perfect to *kill* someone.

After examining the quartz carefully, I put it back on the shelf and again picked up the first one I'd had. Aside from some routine dust, they were clean. I picked up all the quartz rocks in my reach, bending down to get the ones on the bottom shelf, and all of them showed no signs of being a murder weapon. But I couldn't reach the top shelves. The cabinet in the bathroom was too small to house a step ladder, so I walked to the back door.

Opposite the door hung a black curtain I had never noticed before. I grabbed the curtain and was about to pull it back to see if there was a ladder hidden there when I got the weirdest feeling. What if someone was hiding back there? So I held my fist in a defensive pose—I had never hit anything in my life, although I had wanted to hit Eddie more than a few times—and pulled back the curtain quickly so I could take the hider by surprise. Nobody was there, but there was a step ladder—and a cat litter box. So I sneezed.

I carried the ladder to the bookshelf and set it up. Then, I was so certain that I was onto something—Petra had said that Sheriff Billy had not found the murder weapon—that I walked to the front, sat down at my desk, pulled the key from its hiding place, and unlocked my purse. I took out my gloves—they were my good ones, and I hated to use them like this, but I had no choice—and locked the purse back up. When I stood, I remembered to look out the window and the red mustang was gone. That was strange. Why hadn't Eddie come to see me? He had come before in the afternoons, it was true, but if he was right there, then why wouldn't he come in?

Shrugging, I walked to the back. After sliding on the gloves, I systematically checked all the quartz rocks that held the books. I moved the ladder over and checked all those. Nothing. Feeling frustrated, I was starting to think that I was wrong about the whole thing, and that I should just let Sheriff Billy do his job. Then I noticed

Rocky the cat waltzing down the stairs pretty as you please, like he owned the place. As soon as I saw him, I started to sneeze.

I wasn't stupid. I knew that part of this allergy was psychosomatic because every time I saw him I sneezed before the dander even got close. But tell that to my nose. Still on the ladder, the sneeze knocked me off balance. I tried to grab the bookcase, but my hand slipped and hit the books instead. It still steadied me, but something strange happened. Some of the books went back, and some of them didn't. The ones that didn't weren't any bigger than the other ones. I moved them over so I could get a better look.

Looking at what was behind the books almost sent me staggering off the ladder. I didn't need my gloves to pick up the quartz rock. Because I could see clearly that the rock had traces of blood on it. Red blood. Gwen's blood.

CHAPTER TWENTY-EIGHT

IN MY EXCITEMENT of finding the rock, I almost fell off the ladder trying to get to the front. I didn't know the number for the sheriff's station, and although I had the internet in front of me now, I would not waste time looking there. I punched in 9-1-1. I had that number in my head.

"Hello! It's not an emergency, but it's urgent. I need to speak to Sheriff Billy! . . . Okay, thank you." She gave me the number, and I wrote it on the blotter. Then I punched in the new number.

"Sheriff Billy, please. It's urgent." When she asked if I had called 9-1-1, I told her it wasn't that urgent, so she put me through. "Yes, Billy. Guess what? I found the murder weapon! . . . Oh, yeah, sorry. It's Lorry Lockharte at the Rutledge Historical Society. . . . You will? Great. I'll see you soon." I wasn't sure he believed me, but he sounded bored and probably said he'd come over to humor me.

A few minutes later, he stepped through the door. "What's this fantasy about now, Lorry?"

As I stood, I looked up at him. He was tall and

handsome. Too bad he was a cop. I hated their arrogance and power-tripping. "You don't believe me, do you, Sheriff Billy?"

He shrugged. "I was tired of staring at the four walls, so I thought I'd come over to humor you."

See? I was right, so I frowned at him. "Hmmmph. Come on. Follow me."

I marched my little—I mean big—butt into the back room. When I showed him which shelf it was on, he moved the ladder over out of his way and reached his hand in to grab it.

"Wait! Billy, don't touch it! If I'm right, you'll be contaminating evidence!" If he had believed me, he would have known that.

He groaned and moved the ladder back in place. I was standing to the side of him, and when he climbed the ladder and looked at the quartz rock, I saw his eyes go big and round. "Oh! Wow!" He looked down at me, from even farther than he usually looked down at me. "This really could be something." He pushed the button on the radio attached to his shirt. "Yeah, it's me! Send Nick and Derek straight over to the historical society with the kit! Now!"

Nick and Derek must be the two twelve-year-old deputies. And "the kit" would be the forensic kit. I stood there with my arms crossed on my chest and looking smug.

Billy took one more look at the rock before climbing down the ladder. He put his hands on his hips. "I suppose you're pretty proud of yourself for finding this, huh?" I nodded. "Well, Lorry, I'm proud of you, too." Then he did something most unexpected. He hugged me. "Good job, Lorry."

124

"Now will you let Zackary James out of jail?"

"What? Young Zack? This doesn't prove that he didn't do it. You found the murder weapon! We will check it for fingerprints, and I'm sure Zack's will be on there—if we can get any off the rock. Hopefully we can."

"What? Oh, yeah." It occurred to me that he was right. It didn't get Zack off the hook, and if his fingerprints were on the rock, then it would convict him. But I still didn't think it was him. Somehow I had to salvage the situation. "Well, how tall is young Zack?"

"I'd guess five feet nine, why?"

"How tall are you?"

He straightened up before he answered and stuck out his chest. It was kind of cute. "I'm six feet four inches. Why are you asking? What could that have to do with anything?"

"Zack couldn't reach that high."

Billy shrugged. "He could have used the ladder. I'll have the guys check it."

"It was in the back behind a curtain." I motioned over my shoulder.

"He came in the back door. He could have found it."

"Maybe, but if he went to the trouble to get the ladder and hide the rock behind the books, wouldn't it make more sense to take it with him and throw it in the garbage?"

Billy knitted his brow and pinched his lips together. "I'm sure there's a reason."

"Whoever did this was interrupted. He stashed the rock behind the books hoping no one would see it, and he ran out. Zack didn't do it."

"Lorry, honestly, I appreciate your help, but you're not a detective. Let the professionals handle it."

I was sure that Billy was a smart guy and competent, but why couldn't he see what was so obvious? *"The professionals* haven't handled it very well, so far."

"Touché." I heard the front door bell jingle and the door open. "Here are the boys. Just leave it to us."

He patted me on the shoulder and *the boys* stormed in. I had been dismissed.

CHAPTER TWENTY-NINE

IT WAS TOO early to go to lunch, and I couldn't have left Billy and *the boys* there all alone anyway, so I sat at my desk and surfed. When there wasn't anything else to do and I had extra time, I liked looking at houses—not that I could afford to buy even a shack, but it was fun to look and imagine what it might be like if I could afford my own house again. Again. That was funny when it was just weeks ago that I had my own house. And now I don't. How quickly things can change.

Sheriff Billy walked out from the back, and although I heard him coming, I pretended that I didn't. He stood behind me for a few minutes, and I clicked away and kept pretending.

Finally, he spoke. "If you didn't feel me behind you, you'll never make a good cop."

I laughed. "One, who says I didn't feel you behind me? Two, who was it who found the murder weapon?"

He chuckled, patted me on the shoulder, and walked out the door. His patrol car was double parked in front of the historical society. Rutledge was a small town. If someone's car was blocked, they would be just as likely to get into the patrol car and move it themselves. But no one did.

Fifteen minutes later, the boys marched out without acknowledging me. "You're welcome!" I shouted after them. They didn't even realize I was talking to them. They must have thought it was a private conversation with the fish, and they didn't want to interrupt.

After surfing around a little more, I closed the internet browser in disgust. I could barely afford to put gas in my car, and I was looking at houses. It was stupid.

And it was time for lunch—not to eat lunch, I rarely did—but to get my divorce started. Yay. I moved the hands on the *Be Right Back!* sign to one o'clock and hung it on the door. Then I locked up and walked to the back room. There was fingerprint dust *everywhere*. It was much worse than before, and it would take me a while to get it all cleaned up—when I got back.

I drove over to the Town Offices, parked in their lot, and walked inside. The woman at the window, who was talking on her cell phone, directed me to the family court filing counter. The clerk there, who wore a green dress shirt and a black tie, asked to see my identification. When I handed it to him, he compared it to the name on the papers, and then notarized the forms that needed notarizing. Then he asked for the money. I gave him the nearly three hundred fifty dollars in cash that he asked for.

"Will your husband sign the papers willingly?" he asked.

"No, I'm afraid not."

He handed me back two of the forms I had filled out. "Then you'll need to drop these off at the sheriff, so he can serve the papers."

128

"Can I serve them myself?"

The phone on his desk rang, so he answered quickly. "You'll have to ask him that, sorry." And he closed the window, our business finished.

Now I had to drive back to the sheriff's station. It was only down the street, but I wasn't happy about Sheriff Billy knowing my business. I hauled open the sheriff's building door again and walked in to the sound of the buzzer. The same woman I had seen there before, still dressed in turquoise—it must be a uniform—came to the window.

"Hello, again," she said.

That's what I liked about small town living—people remembered you. It made me smile. "Hi! Is Sheriff Billy here?"

She picked up the phone and asked, "What's this regarding?" I showed her the divorce papers. "Oh, you need him to serve the papers. I can just give them to him."

"Well, I was going to ask him if I could do it myself."

"All right." She punched a number on the phone and spoke in it quietly.

She was very agreeable. I liked that. A minute later, Billy came through the door.

"A divorce, huh? Let me see." He looked at the papers I handed him. "There's no address here for the respondent."

"I know. I don't know where he's living now. But I wanted to ask you if I could serve the papers myself. He keeps pestering me, so I know I'll see him again."

He put his hand on my shoulder and looked at me sympathetically. "Now, Lorry, I have to ask this. Have you seen a counselor or a mediator?"

"No, and I'm not interested in being counseled or mediated. The guy is a jerk, and I want out."

"You're sure about this?"

"Positive." I really wasn't positive. When you're separated from someone you had made a commitment to, and even though the situation was bad, it's still hard to make that final decision to end it. Eddie making his phony token attempts to get back together wasn't helping, either. But I was probably as close to positive as I was ever going to get.

"All right. Yes, you can serve him yourself. No problem. Here in Rutledge we try to be accommodating."

I looked at him and tilted my head. "I *grew up here*, Billy."

He stepped back. "Here? You did?" When I nodded, he continued. "I didn't know that. Well, okay, then, here are your papers back."

"Thank you. Goodbye."

"Goodbye, Lorry." He opened the heavy door for me, and I walked out into the parking lot. When I got to my car, I glanced back, and he was still watching me.

CHAPTER THIRTY

NOW I WAS getting paranoid. Why was he watching me? Did he think *I* planted the bloodied rock on the bookshelf? Will he be comparing my fingerprints to the ones on the ladder and the rock? I shook my head and my body like a dog shaking off water and tried to think about something else. That kind of negative thinking wasn't getting me anywhere.

I drove back to the office, parked in the back, walked through the back passage, and groaned at all the fingerprint dust everywhere. It looked much worse from this angle. Since it wasn't time for me to come back from lunch yet, I decided to clean it right there and then. From the bathroom utility closet, I retrieved the dust cloth and the Dust 'N Clean and got right to work. Fifteen minutes later, it was all cleaned, and I felt much better.

After returning the now clean ladder to the back behind the curtain, I replaced the dust cloth and dusting can, put the chain back up, grabbed my purse from the bookshelf where I had left it, and walked toward the front. Someone was at the door walking rapidly back and forth. It was a wonder he didn't wear a hole in the pavement, he was walking so fast and placing his feet so vigorously that I could hear it inside. It wasn't Eddie—the man was too tall for that. When I got to the door to remove the sign and unlock the door, I saw that it was Ezra Yoke, and that made me smile.

I was still smiling as I unlocked the door and opened it, and he raged inside. He glanced around and then looked at me with fire in his eyes. "*Betty* never closed up for lunch!"

I was so taken aback by his words and demeanor that I stepped backward to avoid him and didn't say a thing. A second later, he was smiling again, the warmth back in his eyes, and he reached for my hands. "Oh, I'm so sorry, Lorry. A business deal went wrong this morning, and I took it out on you. So sorry." Ezra brought my hands up to his lips and kissed them both. He looked at me again like I was the only woman in the world, and I fell gratefully into the depths of his eyes.

"I'm so sorry, Ezra." I was about to say it wouldn't happen again, but it might, and I'm not a liar.

He kissed both of my hands again and let them go. "Not a big deal, Lorry. Like I said, bad business." He shook his head. "Now that I'm here, with you, I'm feeling much better."

I wanted to fall into his eyes again, but he had turned away. Not wanting to let that feeling go, I took a step toward him, but it was too late.

"I better get to work up there if I'm going to get anything done." Ezra walked away without another word or another glance. And I just watched him go, enamored once more.

When I got my brains back from my close encounter

of the sensuous kind, I noticed there was a brown envelope on the floor that had been shoved through the mail slot on the door. I picked it up and saw it was more correspondence from Martha. Sitting at my desk, I locked my purse in the bottom drawer and opened the envelope. It was two letters and two documents, but I could almost not make out the writing. It almost looked like it was a foreign language. Martha's previous documents had paid tribute to her careful and clear handwriting, but with these papers, I would have to *translate* them before I ever began to type. And I could tell that it was Martha's handwriting, because she always dotted her "i"s with a line instead of a dot. She must have been in a big hurry when she wrote them.

A half hour later, I had almost finished the translating except for one document. It was several pages long and would probably take me another hour by itself. When I finished that one, there was still one word that I couldn't figure out. I read the sentence over a dozen times, and even the content of the sentence didn't give me any kind of hint. Finally, I realized that I had to call Martha.

I punched in her number and was told that she was out of the office. No problem. I'd type the other documents first. Maybe she was even on her way over here. The trouble was that I'm a fast typist, and in almost no time, I had finished typing the other documents. The undecipherable word was at the end of the final document—a long document, nearly ten pages—so I thought I might as well type what I could read while I waited for her to return.

When I was almost to the last page, I heard Ezra racing down the stairs. He rushed into the room, checking his watch. "I have a business conference call that I forgot about. See you in a day or two!" The bell jingled as the door opened and closed, and he was gone.

I shrugged and kept typing. When I got to the final page—where the unknown word was—I called Martha again. The receptionist said she still wasn't available. "Listen, I'm Lorry Lockharte at the Rutledge Historical Society, and I need to reach her so I can finish this document I'm working on. Could I call her cell or something? It would only take a minute."

"Oh, Lorry! Yes, I heard you were working there now. This is Melissa Domingo!"

"Hello, Melissa." She had been Missy Domingo when we were in school. Missy went out briefly with Tom Patterson and was invited into the group until they discovered that her family rented their home instead of owned it. It's difficult to believe, but yes, that mattered to those snobs.

"Lorry, listen, I'm not supposed to tell anyone, but since you work there, I think I should. Martha is at the hospital in Coyote Moon."

"Is she okay? What's wrong?"

"She's fine. It's Hugo. He's had a heart attack."

CHAPTER THIRTY-ONE

AFTER MAKING DOUBLE sure the unfinished document was backed up, I strode up and down the office wondering what I should do. My gut feeling was to drop everything, lock the place up, and rush over to the hospital to be with Martha. Although I hadn't known her long, she and Hugo had been extremely kind to me, and I felt I should go. But I couldn't just lock the joint up and take off without asking someone first. That didn't seem right. I realized then that I needed Petra's cell number. She would know what I should do. According to the clock on the computer, she should soon arrive. At least I hoped she would.

Twenty more minutes of pacing and Petra arrived. I was on her before she was even in the door.

"Petra! Hugo! You know, Martha's husband! He's in the hospital! He had a heart attack! Should we go over there right now?"

She raised her arms and brought them slowly down, and said, "Breathe. Just breathe. It will calm you down." Petra took me by the shoulders and sat me down in the chair. "*We* can't just leave and close the place down. It's a business. It's a service to the community. You might not have had too many customers since you started, but trust me, you will. And it might be today. When we close, then we can go see Martha and Hugo in the hospital." Then she narrowed her eyes and sunk her head into her shoulders. "Could you maybe give me a ride over there with you?"

"Petra, of course! But are you sure we can't go now?"

Petra shook her head. "No, Lorry. Someone could come in any minute and want to see the exhibits or do some genealogy."

"Genealogy? No one ever told me about that."

"That's because all the books are askew right now with the move upstairs. But anyway, someone could come in any minute." Someone turned away from our view had put his hand on the door. "See? There's someone right now. Aren't you glad we didn't leave?"

The bell on the door jingled and the door opened. When I saw who it was, I said, "No, I'm not glad at all."

It was Eddie, looking all spiffy in black slacks, white shirt with a conservative dark green tie, and patent leather shoes. He put out his arms, probably still expecting me to fall right into them. Not this time, buster. "Aren't you glad to see me?" he asked.

"Frankly, no." Then I got an idea, so I stood up and stood next to him. I put my hand to my head and measured where it came to on him. "Eddie? Can you help me with something?"

"Sure, Truck, anything you want."

Suddenly, being called that derogative term for all these years infuriated me. If one of those quartz rocks had been nearby, I might have brained him with it. Instead, I would take Eddie to the rock. "Come with me,

Eddie!" I walked down the hallway and motioned him to follow with my finger over my shoulder.

"Oooh, you're taking me into your back room. I'm excited."

"Don't get your hopes up too high."

"What is *he* doing back here?" asked Petra as we walked by her desk. "Lorry, he has no business back here! What are you doing?"

Motioning Eddie to follow, I kept walking. After unhooking the *No Admittance* chain, I came to a stop in front of the bookcases. Eddie tried to put his arms around me, and I pushed him away. "Look!" I pointed to the higher book shelves. "How high can you reach?" When he stood on his tiptoes to reach, I pointed and said, "No tiptoes! I want to see how high you can reach." He couldn't reach where the rock had been. Case closed. "Fine. You did great, Eddie, now let's go meet Petra."

Stepping out, I re-hooked the chain and stopped in front of Petra's desk. "Petra," I said in a soft voice that was entirely not my own, "I'd like you to meet my ex-husband, Eddie."

"I'm not your ex-husband! I'm your husband!"

Ignoring him, I said, "Eddie, this is my friend, Petra. Isn't she pretty?" I knew Eddie would like her, tattoos and all.

He took her hands and clasped them in both of his. I thought he would kiss her hand, but he didn't have an ounce of the class that Ezra did. He just held them and gazed lovingly into her eyes. She tried to pull her hands away, and he wouldn't let her.

"Petra, keep him here for a minute, would ya?" I hurried into the other room while I heard Eddie murmuring sweet somethings to Petra.

Looking over my shoulder lest he find my hiding place, I grabbed the key, got my purse out, and pulled the papers from the purse. Then I locked the purse back in the drawer. I returned to Petra's office to find Eddie leaning down toward her ear and she trying to push him bodily away. Trying being the salient word. Eddie was strong.

"Ahem!"

"Oh, hi, Lorry, I was just getting to know your friend Petra better."

"Yes, I bet you were, Eddie. And for yet the millionth lie you've told me, I bequeath upon you this paperwork." I handed him the papers. "And Petra is my witness that you received them." Then I twirled myself around in a circle three times and said, "I divorce you, I divorce you, I divorce you."

"You can't do this! It's not right! I love you, Lorry! You know how much I love you!"

"Sorry, buddy, no more lies. Let me show you to the door." I stepped toward the door, and Eddie reluctantly followed. He still had his eyes on Petra. I opened the door to show him out.

"Wait, Lorry. What about the money you were going to give me?"

"There was no money I was going to give you, Eddie. Now get out! I don't want to see you again until the divorce! Don't come back!"

Eddie scowled and walked out the door. The red mustang was parked two doors down and had that same blond in it. Some things never change.

"Will he come back?"

"Undoubtedly."

"Great move giving him the papers in front of me. By

the way, that womanizer freak asked me out! And when I told him I'd call the police, he said that all police were arrogant and power-tripping jerks. Isn't that what *you* said about them?" I nodded and frowned, and tried to sneak out of the room, but there was nowhere to go. "That was another one of Eddie's influences on you. What else? What else besides the fish and the cops? What else is there that he brainwashed into you?" When I just looked down, she wouldn't let up. "Come on, Lorry, I know there's something. Tell me."

I thought if I put my mind elsewhere, the question would go away. The more I thought about it, as I stood there with my head down, the more I realized that Petra was too stubborn to let it go. She had caught me at something, and she would not let me get away with it. I set my jaw and looked at her. "I'm a chess master," I said quietly.

"You're what? A chess master?" She laughed. "Now you're trying to pull my leg. Come on, tell me the truth."

Shrugging and tilting my head at her, I walked into the other room. The truth had come out, and it wasn't so terrible after all. Of course she hadn't believed me. That was okay, too. I thought that would be the end of it, but she followed me to my desk.

"Lorry, are you serious? You're really a chess master? How freakin' cool is that! Wow! Wait until Mason hears about this!"

I didn't turn around. "Who's Mason?"

"My boyfriend! And he plays chess!" She took a breath and continued, "And did you know that chess originated in India before the seventh century? Some people think it was China, but it's obvious that it was India. It was derived from an Indian game called

139

chaturanga."

I was too tired to respond. It had been a busy day what with filing for divorce, finding the rock, and serving Eddie his papers. Finding the rock! Petra didn't know about that yet. "Petra! Guess what happened today? I found the murder weapon! It was one of those big quartz rocks used as bookends in that bookshelf back there!"

"Seriously?"

"Yup. Sheriff Billy came over and called *the boys* over to do the forensics. There was fingerprint dust everywhere—even more than before." Then I frowned. "But it still doesn't get your friend Zack off, I'm sorry to say. Billy said he expects to find Zack's fingerprints on the rock."

"Crystal."

"What?"

"It's a quartz *crystal*, not a quartz *rock*."

"Oh, okay, whatever. But I was thinking of going over to talk to Zack. How about you come, too? We could go over after the hospital."

"I'll go with you, but I won't go talk to him. I just can't. You can tell me what he says."

Our conversation was interrupted when the bell jingled and the door opened. It was another professional courier, the same guy as before. "I'm looking for Lorry Lockharte."

I raised my hand. "Still me," I said as I stuck out my hand for the envelope.

"Can I see some identification, please?" he asked in a deep voice.

"It's still me!"

"I have a bad memory." He stuck out his hand. "ID, please, ma'am."

After asking said courier to turn around, I retrieved the key and unlocked my purse. It doesn't hurt to be too careful with important keys. When I handed him my driver's license, he took a quick glance, too quick to even read my name, and then handed me the large envelope. "Bye and thank you," I said as he raced out the door.

"What is it?" asked Petra.

I opened the large envelope and pulled out the business size envelope that it contained. "It's from my mother's lawyers," I said. "Again."

"Wow," said Petra. "Open it."

CHAPTER THIRTY-TWO

OPEN IT, SHE said. As if I was going to stand there and stare at it. Wait. That's just what I was doing. Truth was, I was afraid to open it. They had already sent me a check for five hundred dollars for the divorce. Did they know that it didn't cost all of that, and they wanted the rest back? I was counting on that money to put gas in the car. I had given my entire advance to Martha for the rent.

"What are you waiting for?"

Several minutes had gone by while I was pondering. Taking a deep breath, I opened the envelope. I quickly read the letter and then read it a second time.

"Well, what does it say? Do they want the change back from what you paid for the divorce?" Petra was thinking the same thing I was.

"Uh uh." Then I read the letter to her. "*Dear Ms. Lockharte, It has come to our attention that you have completed filing for divorce. To celebrate that auspicious event, enclosed please find a check for five thousand dollars. And when the divorce is final, expect another check from us. If you continue your avoidance of Mr. Edward Keeley after that, you can expect more financial assistance.*

Sincerely—"

"Is there a check in there?" Petra took the envelope out of my hand and found the check. "Wow! Five thousand dollars! You should have divorced Eddie a long time ago!"

"Shhh!" I said, looking around. "Eddie will hear you. He has an uncanny ability to smell money."

Five thousand dollars made out to *me*. Unbelievable. It had been a long time since I thought it was lucky to be me. In all those years with Eddie, I never thought being me was a good thing. Now, I didn't seem so bad. Maybe Petra's prescription for more self-esteem was working. I was the one who found the murder weapon. I guess I wasn't such an idiot—which is what Eddie tried to lead me to believe all those years. Wait. He didn't try, he succeeded. Now I was finally starting to look at myself differently—thanks to a sixteen-year-old kaleidoscope girl. In a moment of spontaneous gratitude, I hugged her.

"What was that for? I didn't give you the money," she said, backing away.

"No, you gave me something better. You made me feel good about myself. Come on, it's five o'clock. Let's go see Martha and Hugo."

Petra locked the door while I put the envelope with its precious contents into my purse. When we went through the chained area, I showed her where I had found the quartz rock—I mean crystal.

"Wow. How did you find it?"

"Well, your friend Rocky helped me."

"I've never seen him on these shelves. He likes the ones upstairs."

I chuckled. "No, not like that. While I was on the

ladder dusting the shelves, Rocky came down the stairs—
and I sneezed. With my eyes closed—in the middle of
the sneeze—I reached for something to grab onto so I
wouldn't fall off the ladder. My hand accidentally
pushed some of the books back. But I thought it was
strange that the books were all the same size but only
some of them got pushed back. When I pulled the books
away, I saw it right away—that is, I saw the blood."

"Oh, yuck."

"So I called Billy, and of course he didn't believe me
until he saw it for himself."

By this time we were sitting in my Karmann Ghia,
and it wouldn't start. Although I didn't want to flood the
engine, I was eager to get to the hospital, so I took my
foot off the gas. A couple more tries, and she started up
just like downtown. We were on our way.

There was no hospital in Rutledge, only an urgent
care facility. Anytime anyone called an ambulance and
something serious was suspected, the ambulance took
them directly to the hospital in Coyote Moon. The
hospital was in the middle of town. Originally, it had
been at the edge of town, but since the casino had been
built, the town had spread out around it.

I parked in the lot across from the handicapped
spaces. As I got out of the car, I saw a car pull into the
space across from me. The man stuck a handicapped
plaque on his rearview mirror, jumped out of the car,
and trotted into the hospital. He was young and healthy.
I hated that. It was the last handicapped space around.
Where can I report that creep? Then I had a more
benevolent thought. Maybe he was running inside
because one of his parents was about to croak. But then
again, why did he have a handicapped plaque in *his* car?

Oh, forget it! I had more important things to worry about in the present moment.

The hospital was a large red brick building in a V configuration. It had four stories and many windows. Petra and I walked past the doctors' parking area—they're healthy, why do they have to park so close, I wondered—and into the main entrance which was next to the emergency entrance. There were bus-type benches along each side of the entrance that had a red plaque in the center that showed a picture of a cigarette with a line through it and said *Thank You. This is a Tobacco Free Campus.* At the door, there was a large red sign that said *Flu Alert! Dear Visitors, If you have a cold or flu symptoms, please do not visit patients!*

It said more but Petra had already opened the door and walked in, so I followed. The interior door had white lettering on the glass that said *Arizona State Law 13-3102 Prohibits Deadly Weapons in this Hospital.* There was also a picture of a gun with a line through it. No guns, no cigarettes, and no flu—this hospital was taking away all our fun.

The front desk reception area had a bouquet of flowers—mostly lilacs and baby's breath—brochures, and an industrial-sized container of hand sanitizer. They must expect a lot of dirty visitors. There was a slight tang of disinfectant common to hospitals. It's possible that it wasn't really there, but I expected to smell it and I did. Or perhaps it was just that a doctor who had been bathed in it had recently walked out the door.

The receptionist told us that Hugo did not have a room assigned yet. He was in intensive care. Petra and I looked at each other in fear. Then she directed us to the intensive care waiting room where we found Martha sitting in a chair staring off into space. Petra ran up to her, but I tried to appear more dignified and walked slowly up to her. I *wasn't* more dignified—which is why I tried to appear that way.

"Oh, Petra! Thank you for coming!" When Martha lifted her head from hugging Petra, she saw me. "Lorry, thank you for coming!" she said with the same sincerity. She reached out a hand and gave mine a brief squeeze.

"How's Hugo?" I asked.

"He was in surgery all afternoon—emergency bypass surgery. He's only been out of surgery for an hour, and the doctor said not to expect him to wake up from anesthesia for a while. And even then, he won't be able to talk, because he has a breathing tube right now." When she saw me grimace at the mention of the breathing tube, she added, "The breathing tube is normal after surgery. Anyway, I go in every few minutes to touch his hand and let him know I'm here for him. But it was so scary! I thought I was going to lose him."

She wrapped her arms around Petra again and tears ran down her cheeks. "We were talking on the phone— he called me because he didn't feel well—and then he gasped and dropped the phone. I called the ambulance immediately, and they brought him here." She sniffed. "The doctor said if I hadn't been on the phone with him and called the ambulance right away, he probably wouldn't have survived." The tears flowed again, then she looked at the clock on the wall. "I need to go see him again now. I don't like to leave him alone for too long, even though he's not awake, because I think he knows when I'm there. So, thank you both for coming. He should be in his own room in a day or two. Bye!" Martha kissed Petra on the cheek and disappeared into the ICU.

CHAPTER THIRTY-THREE

MY CAR STARTED right up, and I felt grateful for that. Hospitals aren't one of my favorite places, so I was eager to leave. Of course, jails aren't one of my favorite places, either, and that's where we were headed next.

"Do you know how to get there?" asked Petra.

"Unfortunately, yes."

"Oh, that's right. I remember you saying that he wrecked your car while he was driving drunk."

"Yes, he got tagged for drunk driving, and I had to bail him out."

"Tagged?"

"Oh, sorry. That's Eddie's euphemism for getting arrested. He said it didn't sound so bad that way."

Petra put her hand on my arm. "Lorry, you have adopted too many bad things from Eddie. Time to let go of him *and* his euphemisms."

"Eddie got *arrested* for drunk driving, and I had to bail him out!"

"Much better!" Petra said with a grin.

I stuck a piece of gum in my mouth and offered one to Petra. She declined. Having bad breath when you're conducting an interview seemed wrong—especially to a young man surrounded by criminals who probably all had bad breath. So my spring fresh flavor should be a welcome respite for him.

The parking lot faced a one-story unobtrusive building. It didn't look big enough to house any inmates, but behind it stood a concrete behemoth that looked exactly like what it was: a moderate security jail. Would I have to go into that concrete monster to see Zack? I shivered. The place gave me the creeps. I didn't want to get close to it even as a visitor. But I came here to get information, so I bucked myself up and strode toward the building like I felt brave. Petra had stayed in the car, so I couldn't even use her for moral support.

When I walked into the Coyote Moon Detention Center, I immediately felt self-conscious and cramped. This was the place where I had paid Eddie's bail and picked him up. It brought back horrible memories. The entry room was tiny. I could barely turn around in it without my big butt hitting a wall. All right, slight exaggeration. But it was small and there was a security camera installed in each corner of the room, whirring with each movement. They moved as I moved, and at the moment, they were all focused on little ole me. They made me feel guilty. I was again ready to confess right then and there.

The receptionist came to the glass window. She must be used to dealing with hardened criminals and their family and friends, because that woman hadn't seen a smile since Kennedy was president. I thought about the contrast between her and the friendly girl at the Rutledge Sheriff's Office. Different people, different places. Coyote Moon had grown into a decent sized city, and with it came city-style crime. No wonder this woman couldn't smile. She wore a white blouse and gray slacks with a black stripe down the sides. Her name tag said Bobbie, which did not fit her unsmiling face. Bobbie asked me to sign the visitor sheet and to give her my identification. Who did I want to see? Zackary James. Was I friend or relative? Friend. She told me to go to station number twelve and then she buzzed me in.

Station number twelve? What was that about? I opened the door, and instead of a line of windows between the visitors and the prisoners, there were about twenty-five computer monitors. Apparently, I didn't have to worry about my breath. When I found station number twelve, I sat down and read the instructions. *Wait for the screen to clear. The prisoner will be with you shortly.* I waited. And waited.

After a long five minutes, the screen focused on a young man in an orange jail uniform. He looked scared and confused. "Hello, Zack. My name is Lorry Lockharte."

"Are you a lawyer?"

"No, I'm sorry. I'm a friend of a friend. Petra."

His eyes lit up. "Petra? Is she here?"

"No, sorry again. Just me. But I assure you she believes in your innocence. Is her belief misguided?"

Zack leaned forward, and despite the computer screen, I was glad that my breath was spring fresh. It was a little disconcerting having him look at me like that. "I didn't do it. I swear it. I told that to the sheriff, and he didn't believe me."

"Why were your fingerprints on the back door?"

"I came to see Petra. Sometimes she works late. I wanted to let her know that I was out again."

The *again* shook me. He looked too young to have even been in jail once. He looked more like he should expect a visit from a truant officer, not a second trip to the county jail.

"Where did you get a key to the building?"

He shook his head. "I didn't have a key. The back door to the cafe is always open, so I came in through there, and opened the door between it and the society."

That surprised me. "So you went in?"

"I stuck my head in. I heard someone dragging something across the floor, so I called softly inside to Petra. But she didn't answer, so I closed the door and left."

"Did you lock it?"

He shook his head. "No, why should I?"

I shrugged. "Good question! So you never stepped inside the historical society?"

Zack leaned backwards and crossed his arms over his chest. "I put one foot in so I could call out to Petra. When she didn't answer, I stepped back. That's all. I never went in. And I *never* killed anybody! Especially *Gwen*. She was always nice to me."

I liked that he was willing to tell the absolute truth—one foot did technically count as stepping inside. "What time was this?"

"Around eight o'clock."

I straightened up in the chair. "Why would you think Petra would be there at eight o'clock in the evening?"

"She often works late there," he said defensively.

"Why?"

He put his head down and wouldn't look at me. "You'll have to ask Petra that."

"Okay, I will." Then I took a breath and recalled

something that Petra told me. I nodded. "Because of her father, right?"

"Yeah, her dad and my dad are *drunks* together at Petey's," he said with disdain. "So she stays at work to keep away from him."

He was talking about Petey's Bar, a sleazy bar the town fathers had yet to run out of town. I admired that Zack was not going to tell me about Petra's father if I didn't already know about him. "All right, Zack. Thank you."

He leaned forward again, and his eyes lit up. "Will you tell Petra hello for me, please?"

Zack was a nice, polite kid. "Yes, Zack, I will." I smiled at him. "And I'll do whatever I can to get you out of here."

"You will? You believe me then?"

"I have no reason not to. You're not lying are you?"

His face became even more serious than before, and he held up his right hand. "No, I'm not lying. I swear it."

I stood up. "I'll do what I can. Bye, Zack." Before I left, I saw him—still on the screen—put his face into his hands.

Returning to the car, I jumped in to see Petra's inquisitive face. "Is he okay?" she asked.

"He's fine—if you can call being in jail fine when you're twelve years old."

"He's not twelve, he's eighteen."

"Whatever. He looks twelve. Zack said he opened the back door—that it wasn't locked—stuck his head in, and called to you. You didn't answer, so he left. What he heard, though, was something being dragged." I looked at Petra. "I think it was Gwen's dead body."

151

CHAPTER THIRTY-FOUR

AFTER DROPPING PETRA off at home, I tooled over to the grocery store to pick up something to fix for dinner. Without Hugo or Martha cooking, I was on my own. But Martha was bound to come home eventually, so I'd make a casserole that would last a few days so she wouldn't have to worry about cooking for herself. It had been many years since I had been to the Rutledge Super Market, and they had expanded in a big way. Everything was in a different place, which, considering when I'd last been there, didn't surprise me. I put my few items—hamburger, noodles, corn, olives, tomato sauce, and cereal for breakfast—on the belt and waited for my turn at the cashier. She looked familiar, and she looked at me like I looked familiar to her, but I couldn't place her, and apparently, she couldn't place me, either.

I opened the door with my key and carried the groceries into the kitchen. Going up the stairs two at a time—carefully as I still had my heels on—I quickly changed into pants, a blouse, and flats, and raced back down the stairs. I really had to start eating lunch, because I was starving.

It didn't take long to figure out where they kept their pots and pans, and I hurriedly set water to boil for the noodles, started browning the hamburger, and preheated the oven to three hundred-fifty degrees. While I kept moving the hamburger around so it would brown evenly, I found and prepared a casserole dish, putting a thick coating of butter on the bottom and sides. If butter is now good for you, then more is better, right? Sounds good to me. When the water boiled, I tossed the noodles in and stirred them while I continued browning the hamburger. As soon as everything finished cooking, I threw it all together in a mixing bowl, poured the mixture into the casserole dish, put it into the oven, and set the timer for thirty-five minutes.

In the refrigerator, I found ingredients to make a satisfying salad and made one. Since I felt so starved, I didn't wait for dinner to be ready to eat the salad, and I shoveled it down. As I ate, I thought about what Zack had told me—about somebody dragging something. He must have disturbed the killer, who then hid the rock behind the books, and hightailed it out the front door— which was why the front door was unlocked the following morning when I arrived for work. After that brilliant deduction, I made my way upstairs while I waited for the buzzer on the stove to sound.

Sitting on the bed, I picked up my purse and took out the letter and the check. I stared at the two items dumbfounded. The check for one thing. What a windfall! Five thousand dollars! It was so much that I didn't even know what to do with it. Yes, I knew exactly what I would do with it. I'd put it in the bank. Second, the letter that promised that I can expect *more financial assistance* if I stay away from Eddie. No problem. I was finished with that slob, now and forever.

Petra was right. Once I felt better about myself, I wasn't as interested in Eddie *The Jerk* Keeley. Maybe nothing would ever come of my investigation into Gwen's death, but at least I was doing something besides working my butt off all day and coming home to Eddie's demeaning rhetoric. *Truck* was officially retired. If he ever called me that name again, I think I would hit him across the mouth. Or maybe in the stomach. No, violence wasn't the answer. Ignoring the jerk would be more effective.

After I had stared at the check and the letter for more time than was necessary, the buzzer downstairs sounded. Glancing again at the two items in my hand and thinking about how doggone lucky I was, I trotted down the stairs, pulled the casserole out of the oven, and sat down at the table by myself to eat. It was delicious as usual. My good friend, Sam Kohn, formerly Sam Katz, shared the recipe —for *Noodle Knoodle*—with me many years ago. I sighed a long sigh and put down the fork while I thought about Sam.

Samantha Katz had moved to Rutledge in my senior year. At the time, I was still grieving my sister's death and was a lost soul. In school, the rich clique didn't want me, and the other major clique in the school—the dopers— would have accepted me, but as depressed as I was, I didn't want to go that route. Interestingly enough, the dopers would have accepted me even if I hadn't partaken in the "goodies," but I didn't trust myself enough to hang with them. So I was a complete loner. Sam changed all that. Most of the teachers seated us alphabetically, so Sam and I were together in five out of six classes. She was open, vivacious, and warm, and her parents had bought a house a few doors down from mine, so they were rich, too—which meant she didn't have to envy me my money.

Sam had no interest in joining the rich clique, which offended Renee Croft so much that Renee constantly tried to sabotage Sam's reputation at school. Sam, who had an A average and was the model student, always somehow managed to one-up Renee. After what happened with my sister, I always thought Sam made the right choice when she moved to the East Coast following high school to attend college. No telling what Renee might have done.

At first, Sam and I wrote all the time. But then she got involved with a boy at school, and I got involved with Eddie. It didn't matter on her end, but from the very beginning, Eddie wanted me all to himself. It wasn't enough that I wasn't dating any other boys, I had to give up all my girlfriends, too—even Sam who was thousands of miles away. Eddie needed to control every single aspect of my life. In the beginning, it felt like he was doing it because he loved me so much, and I liked it. After a while, though, it made me feel restricted. Still, I didn't try to escape Eddie's tight bonds. And Sam and I eventually lost touch. With sadness overcoming me, I finished eating the Noodle Knoodle, mourning the loss of my friendship with Sam.

CHAPTER THIRTY-FIVE

IN THE MORNING when I walked downstairs, I found that Martha had not returned during the night. I fixed myself cereal and toast for breakfast and put the dishes in the dishwasher. Then I retrieved my purse from upstairs, locked the door to the house, and stepped into my car. It started right up, and I drove straight to the historical society, but I parked in front.

Petra was already there, so the door was open. "Morning, Lorry!" She called from the other room. "How come you came in the front?"

I passed by my desk so I could talk to her. "If you'll be here for a while, I'd like to go to the bank when it opens."

"The drive-thru is open now."

"I need to open a new account, and I want to make sure there's no issues with Eddie claiming to be my husband and taking the money out."

"That's a good idea. I can stay till a little after nine. And if you're not back, I'll put the sign on the door."

"I'll make sure I'm back—barring any unforeseen problems. Thanks, Petra."

156

She flicked her hand in the air without looking up. "No worries!"

At five to nine, I said goodbye and slid out the front door. Two minutes later, I parked at the bank and stood by the front door until they opened at nine. Then I walked directly to new accounts, explained the situation, showed the woman a copy of the divorce papers, and implored her to put a note on the account not to release *any* money to Eddie Keeley. Normally, a bank would never do that anyway. But in small towns like Rutledge, rules are often bent or broken. When I left, I felt reasonably certain that my money was safe.

I made it back to the historical society by nine-fifteen, and Petra was just gathering her belongings. "Hey, Petra. How about if we put the sign on the door, and I'll drop you off at school? That way you won't be so late."

I could tell that she was about to say no, then she nodded her head and smiled. "Thank you, Lorry. You'll only be gone five minutes. That will be fine." The fact that she was going to say no told me what a responsible and conscientious girl she was, despite the tattoos and purple hair. I really needed to stop judging people by their appearance or anything else. That was Eddie's deal, not mine. Time to stop.

Upon returning from dropping Petra off, I returned to the historical society and wondered how Hugo was and if Martha was still at the hospital with him. When I checked my email, the only thing there was a forward that Petra sent of cute dog pictures. Yes, they were cute, but they all reminded me of Bingo, so I had to delete the email. I knew I'd never get over missing that dog.

I was about to feel sorry for myself again when Martha walked in, looking tired and disheveled. "Hi,

Lorry. I'm on my way home, but I wanted to stop and let you know Hugo is progressing fine. He's still in ICU, but they're planning to move him to the regular cardiac unit tomorrow if all goes well. And then he'll be there for a week before they release him. Could you let Petra know?"

"Sure, Martha. Of course."

She opened the door to leave and then turned around. "Lorry, I know you didn't know Gwen or Betty, but their funeral is tomorrow, and I would appreciate it if you could attend. It's not mandatory—but it would be nice."

I hated funerals, but I smiled, nodded, and said, "I'll be there, Martha. There's a casserole in the refrigerator if you're hungry. Although, I guess it's a little early for that."

She put her hand on her stomach. "I'm starved for some real food! Casserole sounds perfect. Thanks, Lorry!" And with her usual buoyant step that contradicted her tiredness, she slid out the door.

Trying not to think about the funeral and my obligatory attendance, I decided to think instead about the murder. Now that I was completely convinced of Zack's innocence—I thought he was innocent before, but I had not felt certain—I had to figure out who did the deed. The only suspect I had left was Michael Wellesley, the women's brother, who Petra said lied about when he arrived in town. Maybe at the funeral I would learn more about him.

Since I suspected that Betty, who had died a few days before her sister, was also murdered, that's where I would start. Who had a motive to want both sisters dead? The obvious suspect was Michael Wellesley. But was it too obvious? I headed upstairs to look around. Besides my initial visit with Petra, I hadn't been up there since.

Again I noticed how stable the steps seemed and how solid the handrail was. Although if Betty was carrying a box of books, it would change everything. But I didn't buy that. When I got to the top of the stairs, I hunched over and looked up afraid that Rocky would try his Rocky the Flying Squirrel trick and land on my head. I briefly wondered if that's how he had gotten his name— from flying through the air. Then I remembered that Petra had told me it had to do with Rocky Raccoon. Rocky had hidden himself well, but I was in his domain. So I sneezed.

The bookshelves lining the walls had similar books to those downstairs: books on historic Arizona and Rutledge. The library-like bookshelves in the center of the room were mostly empty. I walked over to the boxes on the floor. There was a narrow path between the boxes and the bookshelves. A quick glance at the binders on the shelves showed "Automobiles," "Children," and "Churches," and the binders in the end box on the floor closest to the stairs showed "People."

The binders in the "People" boxes looked as though they had been rearranged inside the boxes. Looking around, I wondered what handsome Ezra had been doing up here. Perhaps he had gotten lost in the binders —reading about all that history from Rutledge would be fascinating. I reached down to pick up a binder labeled "People," but without opening it, I put it back down—I had more important things to do just then, and I knew I could sit there for hours reading the accounts of people long dead.

When I got to the top of the staircase and looked down, Rocky the cat was trotting up. He gave me a quick meow, walked past, and then gave an extraordinary leap up to a shelf that I couldn't even begin to reach. While I sneezed, I had to admire his athleticism. What a jump!

After descending the stairs and unhooking the chain across the back area, I stepped in and glanced up at the bookshelves on the side. There was only a smattering of books here and there. Proceeding slowly across the floor still looking up, my foot bumped into something soft. So I knew it wasn't one of the boxes of books on the floor. When I looked down, it shocked me to realize I had discovered another body.

CHAPTER THIRTY-SIX

AFTER RAISING MY head and whacking myself on the forehead with my hand for finding another body, I looked down to discover that it was a *small* body, and that the body was *moving*. Thank goodness for that! The little boy sat up and leaned against the box behind him. There was a white binder on the floor on one side of him and a colorful book called *Arizona Highways and Byways* on the other side.

"Hello. Who are you?"

"I'm Aiden," he said while rubbing the sleep out of his eye with one hand. "Who are you?"

"I'm Lorry. What are you doing here?"

"Where's Betty?" He ignored my question.

Since his question was one that I didn't particularly want to get into at that moment or anytime soon, I ignored *his* question. "What are you doing here?"

Then he ignored mine. Again. "Where's Betty?"

I figured we weren't getting anywhere this way, so I had to answer his question, but I didn't have to tell him the whole truth. "She doesn't work here anymore," I said, hoping that he wouldn't ask why.

"Oh. I liked her. She was nice to me."

"I'll be nice to you, too, Aiden. What are you doing here?"

He pointed to the binder. "Looking at the pitchures."

"You mean *pic*-tures." He nodded. "But shouldn't you be in school?" Aiden shrugged and looked away. "All right, Aiden, how about I call your mommy to come pick you up?"

Aiden shook his head. "I don't have a mommy. I'm a foster child."

"Oh?"

"You know, I live with people who take care of me until I can get adopted," he explained thinking I didn't understand.

"All right. Foster child." Then I felt bad for the poor kid and patted him on the top of his cute head. He looked six years old, blond hair that needed a trim, blue eyes, and the longest eyelashes I'd ever seen. I knew women who would kill for eyelashes that long. They looked cute on him, though. He wore a t-shirt that was half tucked in, and blue jeans with a patch on the knee. On his feet were tennis shoes that could have used a facelift and some refurbishing.

Aiden nodded. "That's what I said." He didn't say it with malice or being smart, just like he was stating a fact.

"Okay, then, well, how about if we call your foster mother to come pick you up?"

"No."

"Why not?"

"She's too busy." He shrugged again, indicating that he didn't blame her, but he understood.

"How about if I take you back to school then?"

"When Betty caught me back here, she always let me

162

stay for a while."

"If I let you stay, will you be good?"

"I'm always good. I just want to read, I mean look at the pictures." He pointed to the book beside him.

"All right, you can stay for a *little* while." Starting back to my desk, I turned around to look at him again. He already had the book open, but I didn't see any pictures on the page he was on. "How did you get in here, anyway? You didn't come in the front, and I remember locking the back door."

"From the cafe next door." He meant the Koffee Korner. Apparently "the cafe" is how everyone refers to it. "Their back door is always open."

The same door that Zack had come in, and probably the same door the killer had come in, too. That was provocative. While I was pondering this new information, I heard the bell at the front door jingle, so I walked up there to find Kasey standing there smiling, with her bright yellow uniform on. She reminded me of a canary.

"Hey, cousin! How's the divorce going?"

I hesitated, because I knew what she meant. "You mean am I still going through with it? Yes, I am. I filed the papers yesterday."

She jumped up and down and clapped her hands. "Hooray! Yippee!" Then she flung her arms around me in a big hug. It shocked me, but felt good. It was from the heart. "Congratulations, Lorry. I know it must have been a difficult decision for you."

"After all the things he did to me at the end—and before—it wasn't as difficult as it might have been." I turned around and pointed at my butt. "Is it really as big as a mule's?"

163

Kasey gave me a playful shove. "Of course not, Lorry. You know Eddie was always saying things to put you down."

"He was?" Had he really always done that and I had never noticed it? Was I that blind to his abuse? Apparently, the answer was yes.

She nodded. "From the beginning. That's why your mother couldn't stand him."

That was interesting, because it was my mother who started me on the path to being comfortable with someone putting me down. She always blatantly and consistently favored my sister over me. And after Lauren died, she made it clear it would have been much better had it been me in that car. It wasn't anything she said directly, but it was the way she looked at me when she didn't think I was looking. As I stood there nodding my head and thinking, Kasey put her hand on my arm and continued.

"Oh, Lorry. I know your mom wasn't always fair to you—because of Lauren and all—but she did love you."

I knew I would burst into tears at any second if the conversation continued, so I changed the subject. "Hey, Kasey, do you know a little boy named Aiden?"

"Aiden? Of course." She motioned with her head to the back. "Is he there now?"

"Yeah."

Kasey rushed past me to the back room, and I followed. When Aiden heard the footsteps, he glanced up from the book he was looking at. When he saw Kasey, he jumped up and ran into her arms.

"Kasey!"

"Hello, Aiden. I heard you were here."

"I'm just looking at pictures."

"You know you should be in school." She put him down and put her hands on his shoulders.

Aiden looked down. "I don't like it there."

"I know, but you have to go. Just like every other kid in town. Your brothers and sisters all go to school, don't they?"

He nodded. "It's different for them, though."

"It's probably time for you to go back, now, Aiden. Come on, I'll walk you over there." I put out my hand, and he took it.

The three of us walked toward the front of the building, and I put the sign *Be Right Back!* on the door. "Kasey?" I gave her a questioning glance.

"I'll come over later to talk."

Kasey headed toward the Koffee Korner and Aiden and I—hand in hand—turned the other way and started walking around the historical society's building. When I looked up at it, I noticed several long semi-vertical cracks in the bricks. It made me wonder how stable the building was.

"Lorry?"

I looked down at him and smiled. "Yes, Aiden?"

"It's faster if you go through the building."

"You're probably right, but it's such a beautiful day out. Look at the blue sky and the clouds. Aren't they pretty?"

He looked up, thoughtfully, and turned his head this way and that. "You're right. It's beautiful out here. I've never noticed."

That gave me a pang in my heart, and I picked him up and hugged him. Then I kissed him on the cheek and put him down.

Aiden looked at me and grinned. "I think you like

me!"

He was right. I did like him. A lot.

CHAPTER THIRTY-SEVEN

THE WALK TO school wasn't far, and luckily for Aiden, we needed to cross no streets to get there. It was in a cul-de-sac at the end of Main Street which was the next street over from High, where the historical society sits. The school was a two-story red brick building. Why were schools always red brick? Even the one-room school house, now defunct, was built out of brick. The *new* elementary school that I was walking toward now, used to be the old high school until the new one was built on the other side of town. When I attended school here, it was already the elementary school.

We walked into the front door hand-in-hand. Clean polished floors, just like in the days I went to school there, greeted us. To each side were glassed-in cases of sports awards and pictures of the alumni who had won them. I wasn't there because I was never sports oriented. Why don't they ever have scholastic awards in those places? Not that I would have been there, either, but oh, well.

Straight ahead was the library, and to the right of that was the computer room. That was a storage room in my day. What are computers doing in an elementary school, anyway? Well, I guess in these days of modern technology, even kindergartners need to be computer literate. We turned left to where the office was. When we walked in, I wasn't surprised to see the smiling face of Marylou. She had already been at the school for years when *I* went to school. Marylou was a fixture and *everybody* loved her. I hadn't been there for twenty years or more, but good ole Marylou still recognized me. Marylou was short, petite, dark hair, dark eyes, and always a ready smile. Today she wore blue capris with a white blouse tucked in and the sleeves rolled up. Warmth emanated from her, and anyone anywhere close to Marylou could feel that warmth wrapped around them. She was awesome.

"Hi, Lorry! Who do you have there?"

Aiden, not waiting for an invitation, charged through the swinging door to the back of the office, and flew through the air into Marylou's waiting arms. "It's Aiden, Marylou! *You* know that!"

"Indeed, I do, Aiden, indeed I do," Marylou hugged him tight until Aiden squirmed out of her arms.

Aiden pointed toward me. "Lorry is my new friend, Marylou. She's nice to me."

"Well, guess what, Aiden? Lorry is *my* friend, too!" Then Marylou looked at me. "Thanks so much for bringing him back, Lorry! Heard you are at the historical society now. You like it?"

This nostalgia was taking me places I didn't want to go. When my father died, the principal was out of town, and telling me that my father died fell upon Marylou. She told me later that my mother had called her crying and begging her to tell me because she didn't have the heart to. I never forgave my mother for that, and I have felt gratitude for Marylou ever since. "So far, so good."

She picked Aiden up again. "Well, we need to get you back to class, don't we, big guy?" Marylou kissed his cheek. "Nice seeing you, Lorry. Stop by again sometime."

I knew I'd never be able to repay Marylou for her kindness all those years ago, but in my heart, I knew that she understood that. She did favors for everyone—students and teachers alike—and expected nothing in return. There was no one like Marylou, and I loved her. I smiled, nodded, and walked out the door.

After I dropped Aiden off, I hurried back to the historical society, pulled the sign off the door, and sat back at my desk. Before I could collect my thoughts, the bell on the door jingled and in walked a woman, all smiles.

"Hi, Lorry!" She threw her arms around me and gave me a hug.

"Hiiiii, ah—" I couldn't remember her name, and I hoped she didn't notice. The woman, like Renee Croft, had what Eddie called an hourglass figure. Eddie always wanted me to have one, but I wasn't the hourglass-figure kind of girl. It looked good on what's-her-name. She wore a pastel pink and yellow print dress with shoes and purse to match. She had been in the doper clique in high school, but she had definitely cleaned herself up.

"Kasey told me you were back in town and working here now." Then she opened the door, leaned over, and gave me another brief hug. "It's been good to see you, but I gotta run! Bye!"

"Goodbye," I said as she closed the door.

Then the bell jingled again, and Kasey strolled in.

"This is my ten-minute break, so I have to hurry, but here is the story on Aiden. He lives in a foster home with nine other children."

"Oh! No wonder he said his foster mother was too busy to come get him."

Kasey nodded. "Yes, that's why. But as far as school is concerned, he's in special education and really struggles there. He refuses to read, and his regular teacher and his reading teacher have been trying everything they can think of to get him interested in reading."

I thought about him and the white binder in the back —but he said he was looking at the pictures. There was also the Arizona book, so I didn't mention it to Kasey.

"When Betty was here, poor thing, he would come and visit and look at the books in the back. She would let him stay a while and then would walk him back to school."

"So he was telling the truth when he said she'd let him stay here for a while."

Kasey nodded again. "Oh, yeah. Aiden *always* tells the truth. Anyway, that's the story! Bye!"

And before I could say another thing, she was out the door, and I was alone again, thinking about Aiden. He lived with nine other children in a foster home. Even if it was a loving place—and I had no reason to believe it wasn't—how much attention could he have from his foster parents with that many kids around? Not much, I was sure. What was the possibility of *me* adopting him? Oh, it was a silly idea for me to even consider. I was in no position to adopt a kid. And a kid needing special education? Would I even be cut out for something like that? I wasn't sure. What a great kid he was, though. I liked him a lot.

Eddie never wanted children, and like everything else, I went along with him and thought that's what I wanted, too. Thinking about it now, I *did* want children.

And if the letter from the attorneys was telling the truth about *giving me more financial assistance* if I stayed away from Eddie, then I would be all set. Then I could support a child with no problem. Were the attorneys telling the truth, though? It wasn't like I had no reason to doubt them—I *did* have reason to doubt them. When my mother died several years ago, those same attorneys told me that all her money had gone to charity and that she had disowned me. But now, they had already given me fifty-five hundred dollars. I shook my head. It wasn't like I could adopt him any time soon, anyway.

Although I expected nothing, I checked my email anyway. I was right. Nothing. Nobody likes me, everybody hates me, I'm going to eat some worms. No, I'm not; I hate worms. Not that I've ever tried them, but surely, I wouldn't like them. And worms made me think of the fish tank behind me. I had not availed myself of its pleasures all day. Turning in the chair, I let myself sink into the fishes' relaxing movements. One of the Oranda goldfish briefly chased a smaller Black Moor, which made me smile. And then I wondered who was taking care of the fish. I had never seen Petra feed them, and yet they seemed happy and satisfied.

Petra walked in then, and I asked, "Petra, who takes care of the fish?"

She laughed. "It took you this long to ask? *I* do! First thing when I come in. If I know I will be late, I feed them extra the night before. So you like them again?"

I smiled, not at Petra, but at the fish. "I don't think I ever stopped liking them. Eddie just had me believing that I didn't."

"That sounds about right," she said.

Then we both heard a loud sound. A big motorcycle with a pony-tailed man parked just outside the door. As he walked toward the door of the historical society, I saw the tattoos on his arms. He wore blue jeans, a light blue work shirt with the sleeves rolled up, and a denim vest over that. I expected to see *Hell's Angels* written on the vest, but instead there were Greek letters. What did that mean, I wondered. Whatever. When I glanced over at Petra, I saw that the smile on her face could not get any bigger. The door jingled and opened, and the man walked into Petra's open arms. I had been right. Her boyfriend was a tattooed-up biker.

CHAPTER THIRTY-EIGHT

"LORRY, I'D LIKE you to meet my boyfriend, Mason. Mason, this is my friend Lorry. She works here now." He stuck out his hand and shook mine. He had a firm shake. Mason was tall and rail-thin, in an attractive kind of way. His dark eyes looked good with his dark blond hair. She had picked a looker, all right.

"I hear you're a chess master. Maybe next time I come down, we can play some chess, huh? I'm pretty good myself—although no master."

"You don't waste time telling my secrets, do you, Petra?" I glared at her and then smiled at Mason. "Sure. Why not? It might not be much of a contest. I haven't played in more than ten years."

"Ah, it's like riding a bicycle! I'm sure you'll be back in form in no time! After I beat you a couple of times, you're sure to catch on!"

I nodded to Petra without smiling. "Your boyfriend is funny, Petra."

She looked up at him adoringly. "That's one of the things I love about him. Come on, Mason." And she led him into her small office. I could hear their voices, but

173

they were speaking so quietly, that I couldn't understand the words. It's a good thing because they were probably talking about drugs. I knew that Petra was responsible and reliable, but couldn't you be a druggie and be those things, too? Perhaps not. Maybe they were talking about motorcycles and tattoos instead.

After five minutes of sitting there and trying not to listen to their conversation, I decided that I should go in the back and continue my investigation. Before I had literally stumbled over the cute Aiden, I wanted to look at the books and boxes. I walked by Petra and Mason, trying not to notice that he was sitting in her chair, she was sitting on his lap, and they were kissing. It was hard not to notice. Briefly I wondered if he was a good kisser, and then would have slapped myself in the face for the thought, but I knew I couldn't get any leverage.

I walked past the chain that was hanging down since I had neglected to put it back up when I walked Aiden out. Standing there with one arm across my chest, my elbow resting on that arm, and one finger crooked at the edge of my lips, I thought I must look pretty studious. But looking studious doesn't equate to figuring something out.

I picked up the binder that Aiden had been looking at that was labeled "Taped Interviews." When I opened it, it was all transcribed. There were no pictures in the entire binder, but the story that I happened to turn to in it, about Marilyn Russet, sounded extremely interesting. She had come in a covered wagon in the 1800s with her parents and younger brother. On the journey, the brother had died of dysentery. Oh, stop! Put it down!

After silently yelling at myself to stop reading and start investigating, I laid the book back onto the top of the box where Aiden had left it. Then I looked at the boxes of binders—all of them labeled "Taped Interviews"— and then I looked at the box behind me that Betty had *allegedly* been trying to carry upstairs. All the binders in there, that had been thrown in haphazardly, were labeled "Timeline." There was something here, I could *feel* it.

Walking to the boxes toward the back door, I noticed the dust on the floor indicated there had been more boxes, but they had been moved. Those were probably the ones upstairs. As I walked back, I read the labels on the binders as I went. The first box, closest to the back, contained binders labeled "Police Beat." The next box was partially "Rutledge Public Library" and "Rutledge Post Office" and underneath those binders were more binders labeled "Rutledge Fires" and "Rutledge Chamber of Commerce." In the next box was "Streets and Roads"—they must have had more back then, because they filled the whole box—and the last box was the "Taped Interviews" box.

I moved the box that Betty had allegedly been carrying—without organizing it—next to the other one. Moving back into my standing thinker position, I felt like something was amiss—that I was missing something. That thought made me laugh. Out loud. Which elicited a response from the other room.

"You know what they say," said Mason, "when you laugh at your own jokes, it's the first sign of senility!" Then he and Petra laughed.

"A real comedian, aren't you, Mason?" I called toward them. They both laughed again.

The interruption didn't disturb my concentration. The next step was looking at the boxes and binders upstairs. So I tromped upstairs trying to be loud enough to drown out their laughter. Rocky was stretching from his high perch. I shook a finger at him. "Don't you dare, big boy!" To which he responded, "Meow!" Then he jumped down beside me and walked arrogantly down the stairs.

Before I had a chance to check the boxes on the floor, I heard Petra call me from the bottom of the stairs. When I walked over there, I looked down and saw Petra and Mason standing at the bottom looking up, and Petra was holding Rocky in her arms. I sneezed and said, "What!"

"Time to go home, Lorry. You've worked enough for today." Petra stroked the cat as she talked.

"I just want to—"

"Come on, Lorry, time to leave!" Mason chimed in.

"Give me a few minutes. I think I'm onto something here. Don't worry, I'll lock up."

"We've already locked up. We were wondering if you could give us a ride to my house. Remember it's not far." The cat jumped out of her arms and ran up the stairs toward me. I sneezed again.

"Why? Mason's bike is out front. Take that!"

"Please, Lorry. And we were wondering if we could go with you to the funeral tomorrow."

Resigned, I walked downstairs. "All right. Let's go. I have to get my purse."

I slid into the Karmann Ghia, and Mason sat in the front seat—there was no way he would fit in the back—and Petra climbed onto his lap. They kissed all the way to Petra's house.

When they got out, Petra leaned into the window that Mason had rolled down. "You'll pick us up at 10:45, then? The service is at 11:00."

"Only if you promise not to kiss on the way there."

Petra and Mason, who had also heard the comment, both laughed. "You're just jealous," said Petra as they walked away holding hands.

She was right. I was.

CHAPTER THIRTY-NINE

PETRA'S HOUSE WAS on the *poor* side of town, which was ironic, because it was on the same side of town as the *rich* part of town—only a few blocks over. But Rutledge was a small town like other small towns where the rich and poor live almost arm in arm and still resent each other. Her house was a light green cape cod with dark green trim. And it needed painting. Badly. The yard was a mass of weeds with a cactus sticking up here and there. It might have originally been Arizona xeriscaping, but it had been a long time since anyone had taken care of it, and the weeds overran everything else. As I drove away and looked in the rearview mirror, Petra and Mason had turned around, and they were waving to me. So I flashed them—you know, with my brake lights—and then drove home to Martha's house.

She wasn't there, but had been. I could tell because there was a plate in the sink with remains of Noodle Knoodle on it. Luckily, there was still casserole left, because I didn't feel like cooking again. Besides, there wasn't much else in the house to eat, and I didn't feel like going shopping. I didn't realize how convenient it was to have someone cook for me. Eddie never did. If I didn't cook, he'd order pizza or takeout, and if they wouldn't deliver, he'd send me to pick it up. Thinking about some of the things he did to me, I can't believe I willingly stayed with him for so long. How stupid could I have been?

After dinner, I cleaned up the kitchen and returned to my room. Then I read the time-travel romance book for the rest of the evening, and before I went to sleep, I got my clothes ready for the following day. Most of my clothes were still in the storage locker, but I had fortunately kept out a black dress. It was a sleek little number that was a little too fancy for a funeral, but it was the only black dress I had. And of course, I had black heels to match. I had bought the dress for the one fancy party that Eddie and I were invited to.

And just like Eddie, he got hung up at the casino, and didn't get home until way too late to attend, although he knew I had been looking forward to it. I was angry at him, but he had won at the casino and brought me a beautiful cardigan sweater. That was his way. Let me down and then build me up so I couldn't be mad at him. Was I really involved with that jerk for more than ten years? What an idiot I was.

The following morning, after eating a quick breakfast and getting dressed, I walked out to the car hoping the thing would start. It did. I drove over to Petra's place, and she and Mason were waiting outside for me. She was dressed in a conservative plain black dress, and he wore a black suit with a white shirt and dark blue tie.

"You both clean up well," I said as they stepped into the car.

Mason got in first and Petra looked in. "I know you

179

don't want us to kiss, but you're not going to make me sit back there"—she motioned toward the nearly nonexistent back seat—"are you?"

"No, no. Sit on his lap. That's fine."

Petra, squished on Mason's lap because even the front seat of a Karmann Ghia wasn't that roomy, asked, "You know how to get there?"

"I grew up here! Remember?"

"Oh, yeah." Petra looked at Mason, and I saw her roll her eyes. "She grew up here," she repeated to him in a snarky voice.

"Petra, behave, or I'll kick you out of here!"

"Whaaaat? Me?" And then she and Mason both laughed.

Just when I started thinking of her as almost a grown-up, she pulled something like that. She was only sixteen years old, and she looked like a kaleidoscope. It shouldn't be difficult remembering that she wasn't an adult. Of course, what had being an adult done for me? Absolutely nada. That's *nothing* for those of you who don't know español.

The funeral was held at Rutledge Community Church. I hadn't been there in years. It was a large brown brick building with arched stained glass windows and an arched doorway with etched copper doors. The largest part of the church—the chapel—had a peaked roof, and next to that, a bell tower—still one of my favorite parts of Rutledge—and then the smaller flat-roofed office area on the right.

I parked in the parking lot which was half-full, and we left the car and walked inside, me in front, Petra and Mason following behind talking and holding hands. But I wasn't going to criticize Petra for that. At least she was going. It was a lot more than other sixteen-year-olds might do. Although she was still a kid, she was a good kid.

I hated funerals. I hadn't been to many, but I found them to be depressing, somber affairs. Did the dead really care if you went to their funerals or not? Ponder that question for a while. I didn't think so, but perhaps funerals were for the living. But I got lucky this time. The doors to the chapel were closed, and a large sign with dark blue letters said *Celebration of Life* with a big arrow pointing to the right. I turned to Petra, who had come up behind me. "Did you know it wasn't a traditional funeral?"

Petra shrugged. "Nope."

I knew what was behind the sign, though, in the chapel. It had dark brown carpeting, different from the rest of the church which showed off its real wood floors. Rows of crisp, white pews with dark brown wood trim led up to the pulpit at the front. Behind the pulpit was a large, round stained glass window with a candle in the center. There wasn't much religious iconography in this church because it served so many. For a long time it was the only religious center in town and had to serve all religions.

As I looked down the hallway the way the arrow pointed, I saw a room toward the right with Michael Wellesley standing outside welcoming people inside. I slowed and moved to the side so Petra and Mason could walk in front of me. Before I got to that doorway, I had to figure out what to say. I didn't think "Sorry your sisters croaked, I didn't know 'em anyway" would be appropriate. Neither would "I replaced your sister at the Rutledge Historical Society. Bummer." It wasn't the easiest position to be in—that is, attending a funeral for two people you have never met. Unless you can consider that I met Gwen when I stumbled upon her corpse. But I didn't think that would count.

We got to the door, and Petra introduced Mason, and they both said how wonderful both sisters were. Then they walked on, and it was my turn.

Michael Wellesley, the number one and only suspect in my investigation, wore a black suit, white shirt, and blue and gray striped tie. His eyes looked sad—not in mourning, but the kind of sad that was always there—because of their shape. Aside from the eyes, though, there was an aura of sadness about him. Did he look remorseful or just sad? Could you tell something like that?

When he took my hand in both of his, I said, "My name is Lorry Lockharte. We met at the historical society a few days ago. I'm so sorry for your loss." He blinked away tears in his eyes, nodded, and let go of my hand. Were the tears fake? I didn't know.

CHAPTER FORTY

I WALKED INTO the meeting room, which I hadn't
been in for years and years, but it looked the same. A
bulletin board on the left-hand side as you came in, a
stage with a brown curtain at the far side of the room, a
door to a kitchen at the other side, and brown tied-back
curtains covering the several windows. A white screen
had been pulled down in front of the stage curtain, and
images of Gwen and Betty were shown in a slideshow.
Pictures of them from childhood to adult and old age
were taking their turns on the screen. Why wasn't there
any food set up? Don't these affairs usually include food?
I hadn't had much breakfast, and I was hungry.

Rows of chairs were set up facing the stage, with a
podium set up in front of the curtain. Petra and Mason
had already sat down and didn't leave a seat for me. But
sitting toward the back, I recognized Martha, and so I sat
down next to her.

"Hi, Martha."

"Oh, hi, Lorry. Thanks so much for coming. I hope it
wasn't an inconvenience."

"No, not at all." I didn't mention how I even hated

funerals of people that I *did* know. This wasn't a funeral, though, so maybe it wouldn't be so bad. "How's Hugo? Is he all right?"

She nodded. "He will be. Doctors said he is out of danger now. He's in his own room, tubes removed, and is breathing and eating on his own. He'll be fine, but he'll —well, *we'll*—have to make changes in his diet and in his activities." She turned toward me. "Do you know what the cardiologist told us? He said that he might go down to the cafeteria to have a muffin, but sugar and sweets have been implicated in heart disease! Can you imagine that? Anyway, we're changing our eating habits. If he keeps improving, he'll be able to come home in a week." Martha put her hand on my arm. "I'm so relieved. I was so afraid I was going to lose him."

Before I answered, someone sat down beside Martha on the other side. "Hello, Martha, Lorry." It was Sheriff Billy, not in uniform, but looking his best. And then the Celebration of Life began.

Michael Wellesley took his place behind the podium. The din of quiet conversation in the nearly full room stopped, and the room became deathly silent. That thought almost sent me into a fit of giggles, but I bit my lower lip to suppress my laughter.

"Most of you know me, but for those who might not, my name is Michael Wellesley, and I'm Gwen and Betty Wellesley's younger brother. Welcome to their Celebration of Life." He paused for a moment as if to contain his emotions and then he continued. "It is what each of them requested instead of a funeral. Anyone who wants to is welcome to speak, but we have a few people first who have already asked." He looked our way. "Martha?"

Martha stood up, and I stood up to let her pass into the aisle. Sheriff Billy moved over next to me.

"Hi, Lorry. Thanks for coming. I know that you didn't know either Gwen or Betty."

I shrugged. "Martha asked me to come."

He shook his head. "Doesn't matter. You came. That was very kind of you."

By then, Martha had reached the podium and began speaking. First she spoke about Betty, who had a degree in Library Science and had worked at the Rutledge Historical Society for forty years. Gwen, also had a degree in Library Science, and had worked at the Rutledge Public Library for thirty-five years before retiring and volunteering all over town. I probably would have recognized her if she hadn't been so pale and stiff when I found her. I used to hang out at the library when I was in high school.

Both sisters had been engaged to Marines in the late sixties, and both marines had died in Viet Nam. Neither sister had ever married. Martha spoke about how wonderfully kind and compassionate both sisters were, how everyone in town would miss them, and how much she loved them both. When she finished, she paused for a second, took a deep breath, looked our way and said, "Sheriff Billy."

I moved over so Billy could exit and Martha could sit back down. Billy started by telling many of the good deeds that each of the sisters had done for Rutledge. Apparently they had both been influential in town when they were young.

He told one funny story about how they had set up a fake jail in Rutledge Park for a festival, and the two sisters had agreed to be "incarcerated" until the town had raised a certain amount of money. They were a humorous pair, Billy said, dressed in striped clothing and banging on the bars and yelling at people to let them out. The deal was they wouldn't leave the jail until the money was received—and not leaving included spending the night if necessary. It was nine o'clock at night and still the money wasn't raised. The two women were cold and wanted to go home, but they agreed to stay and they intended to. At nine-thirty, when people were talking about loaning them sleeping bags, Billy finally donated the money himself so they could go home. He didn't tell *that* part of the story—Martha whispered it to me.

Several other people followed Billy, including, surprisingly enough, Petra speaking about working with Betty and enjoying Gwen's visits. She was a good speaker and did a good job. When nobody else stood up, Michael Wellesley stood at the podium again, and told about childhood incidents, growing up, and their relationship as adults. He was an attractive man, and this wasn't his first time behind a podium. He had that natural command of his audience like a seasoned emcee.

When everything was finished and everyone stood up, Martha grabbed my arm. "You're going to the house, aren't you? They'll have food set up there. It will be nice. Please come."

We were walking out the front door of the church by now, and Billy walked around and slipped his arm through mine. "Of course, she'll come! Won't you, Lorry?"

How could I say no to the cute local sheriff? And besides, I was hungry.

CHAPTER FORTY-ONE

SINCE I WAS sitting toward the back of the room and left right after the service, I was able to get a decent parking place across the street and a few doors down from the Wellesley house. I ended up driving over there by myself, because Petra and Mason got a ride from friends they had run into at the funeral—er, Celebration of Life.

The Wellesleys' home turned out to be on Seagate Avenue only a couple of blocks from Martha's. Where the gate was or even the sea was beyond me, but there it was. It was a tall, cheery yellow Victorian house with white trim. Three steps led up to a shiny wooden door with an oval etched glass window in the upper center. The front porch had a white wooden railing like a picket fence, and two wooden rocking chairs blowing slightly in the wind as if there were two people rocking away. Maybe there were. There was a big front window downstairs, and four windows upstairs, all rectangular, two big and two small ones above them.

I walked up the steps and into the house. The front door was open. It smelled like an old person's house. I'm not sure what that smell is or why I associate it with old people, but it smelled homey and comfortable. The room opened into a spacious living room with a wraparound couch, two easy chairs, two more wooden rocking chairs identical to the ones outside on the porch, and several other chairs that had been set up. Light from the windows flooded the room. And there were flowers everywhere. The dining room at the other end had tables set up with an assortment of catered food. There were mini-sandwiches as well as cold cuts and bread to make your own. Mostly chocolate mini-desserts covered one side of the table.

There were only a few people in the room, including Martha, who was in deep conversation with Michael Wellesley. The handsome Sheriff Billy hadn't arrived yet. It was funny. After I left Eddie, I figured I was through with men for life, and here I was attracted to two men. Sheriff Billy, though he's a cop, was not in any way arrogant and power-hungry. Petra was right; I carried too many of Eddie's prejudices. And the debonair Ezra Yoke who looked into my eyes and made me feel like I was the only woman in the world. The thought of him almost made me swoon my way into the chocolate desserts, so I stepped away from the table.

Across from the food was a memory table with photographs and scrapbooks showing the three children —Betty, Gwen, and Michael—growing up. There was a first edition *Huckleberry Finn* on the table and a candy striper vest. As I was pondering the meaning of these items, Sheriff Billy came up behind me.

"Wondering about these?" He pointed to the book and the vest.

"Yup." I loved it when I could be eloquent.

"Betty had a collection of first edition books." He picked up *Huckleberry Finn*. "This was her favorite." While still holding ole Huck, he pointed to the candy striper vest. "Gwen was fond of saying she was the oldest candy striper at the hospital." Billy shook his head. "I will miss them. This town will miss them." He sniffled.

I thought maybe he would burst into tears right there in front of me when Petra walked up. "Hey, Billy!"

"Petra, my girl!" He put one arm around her and crunched her next to him.

Mason walked up, grabbed Petra away, and gave Billy's chest a shove. "What you doin' with my girl?"

Billy's face lit up, and he grabbed Mason and hugged him. "Mason! I didn't know you'd be here! Great to see you! How's school?"

Mason nodded. "Going well."

"Have you cut up any dead bodies yet?" Billy looked at me and put one hand on Mason's shoulder. "My boy here is going to med school!" he said proudly.

Mason shook his head. "Not this year. Probably next."

"Well, I better start mingling. Great to see you, Mason." Billy shook Mason's hand, kissed Petra's cheek, and squeezed my arm. "See you later, Lorry." Then he walked away.

"Oh, Lorry, you have an admirer," said Petra.

"Who? What are you talking about?"

"Sheriff Billy. He likes you."

"Oh, he does not. What makes you say something like that?"

"The way he looks at you—with stars in his eyes." She tilted her head and smiled at me. "He so likes you!"

"Oh, Petra, that's ridiculous! You're making things up!" I was so frustrated that I walked away, leaving her and Mason giggling behind me. She could be so *juvenile*.

The house had filled with people and despite the size of the rooms, it began to feel crowded. I wasn't claustrophobic, but I didn't like to feel that I couldn't *escape*. Escape from what, I didn't know. But regardless, I didn't like the feeling. I saw some people I knew from high school and walked over to talk to them. I knew them, but not well enough that I could remember their names. Ah, well. When the conversation progressed to my marital status, I gave a brief rendition of the end of my marriage and then sauntered off before they could ask for more details.

Suddenly, I remembered something. Don't murderers always go to their victim's funeral? I had forgotten to look when we were at the Celebration of Life, but maybe he or she would be here. Narrowing my eyes, I looked around carefully, trying to be as discerning as possible. What about that man over there? That woman across from him? What about those two at the food table? Is that your second dessert? Someone who would be so crass as to take two desserts could certainly be a murderer. That got me to thinking. I hadn't had a first yet, and two desserts *did* sound good.

Still assessing the murderous capability of each person I came across, I made my way back to the dessert table. I had loaded a plate with the *two* requisite desserts when Billy came over.

He leaned over and whispered in my ear. "I saw you watching the crowd. Don't tell me you're searching for the murderer here." I looked at him with eyes wide, which he took for a confession. "It's a cliche. Sometimes they do, sometimes they don't. It's a device to quicken the plot in movies and novels, not in real life. So you can stop looking."

I took a step back and looked at him. Maybe that's why he got teary-eyed at the memory table—in remorse. Maybe Sheriff Billy was the murderer.

CHAPTER FORTY-TWO

I DIDN'T REALLY think that Sheriff Billy was the murderer. What were the chances? Eddie would have thought there were a lot of chances, but I wanted to get away from Eddie's way of thinking—far away. So I decided to believe in the innocence of the law establishment. Sure there were corrupt cops, but I honestly didn't think that Billy was one of them. I had no reason to suspect him, anyway, besides that it would be my luck to fall for a dirty cop. No, I had to stop thinking that way. Since leaving Eddie, my luck had changed. It would be my luck to fall for a *good* cop.

But right then, I wasn't falling for anyone. I said my goodbyes to the few people whom I knew at the party, reiterated my "sorry for your loss" to Michael Wellesley, and slipped out the door and drove home.

There was still the rest of the weekend for me to contend with. It wasn't that I didn't like weekends, I did, but when I was with Eddie, we were always doing something. Doing doing doing and rarely staying home a minute. *Not* doing something was something that I liked, but it was still unfamiliar, and I wasn't sure what to do with it.

So I did my laundry, and when I found a vacuum cleaner and cleaning supplies in the laundry room, I decided that I would help Martha out. So I vacuumed the entire downstairs and all the rooms upstairs except Martha and Hugo's bedroom. Then I dusted everywhere as well. Since I didn't know if Martha was coming home from the party or going directly back to the hospital, I cleaned the bathrooms, too. It gave me something to do and made me feel useful. The kitchen was already mostly clean, because I had been cleaning as I cooked in there.

When the laundry and the cleaning were all finished, I retired upstairs to my room. I folded and put the clothing away and read a couple of chapters before turning on my computer. Aiden had crossed my mind now and then, and I wondered if I could really pursue adopting him. First, I'd have to have my own place, so I checked Craigslist and the weekly *Rutledge Chronicle* online to see if there was anything available that would suit one lonely woman and a cute little boy. There were a few places, but it seemed like a fantasy, so I never followed up on any of the leads.

Martha came home for a brief time on Sunday to pick up and drop off some clothes. She knocked at my door to let me know that since Hugo was doing so well, she'd be working the following day, and since she was so behind, she'd need a lot of typing done. That was just as well. If I wasn't working, then I spent too much time fabricating who had murdered Gwen and possibly Betty —though I still had no evidence that Betty was murdered. I did however have strong reservations about her falling down the stairs carrying that *big* box.

Monday morning when I got to work, Petra and

Mason were there already. As I walked by Petra's desk, she stopped me. "Lorry! Guess what! Mason knows the guy at Rutledge Taxi!"

I shrugged. "So?" It sounded so irrelevant that I drew out the *so* to two or three syllables.

"*That's* how Michael Wellesley got here! We can find out when he *really* arrived."

"All right. Let me know." For some reason, the whole thing had lost its fascination for me, and I just wanted to get the typing done. Of course, it hadn't lost *all* its fascination, because the reason I wanted to get the typing done was so I could follow up on my lead with the books. I wasn't going to tell Petra that though. I'd let her think I'd lost interest. But the more I felt convinced that both sisters had been killed, the less likely it was that Michael Wellesley had done it.

"Oh, Lorry! You're impossible!" Petra went back to kissing Mason, and I walked to my desk where there was a folder of the typing that Martha wanted.

A minute later, Petra and Mason were at the front door. "I'll see you later, Lorry. Mason has to drive back to school now."

"Bye, Mason." I smiled at him. He was wearing the same clothes I had seen on him the day we met, but I had new respect for him now that I knew he was a medical student. Which was absurd, I knew, but I couldn't help myself. No, I have to stop saying that I can't. Yes, I *can* help myself.

Besides, there are those bikers down in Phoenix—they might even be Hell's Angels—who protect children when they go to child abuse trials. Before the bikers stepped in, the children would be afraid to testify against their abusers, but with the bikers, the children felt safe and protected. Yes, I definitely needed to stop being so judgmental.

"Hey, Lorry. Next time I come down, we'll play some chess, all right?"

"Yes, Mason. That sounds good, but I told you, I'm awful rusty."

Mason smiled and nodded. "That's all right. I'll give you a handicap!" And he slid out the door with his arm around Petra.

Then I sneezed, and then the phone rang. And thus the onslaught of the morning began.

CHAPTER FORTY-THREE

EXACTLY THREE PEOPLE had come into the historical society to see the exhibits since I had started the previous Monday. And I couldn't remember how many times the phone had even rung, but I thought I could count it on one hand. So it was a great surprise when the phone started ringing as soon as Petra was out the door, and then a couple walked in the door. I had to hold one finger up to them to wait while I got off the phone. Then, because I didn't remember putting the *No Admittance* chain back up, I walked in front of them down the hallway. I was right, it wasn't up. After fastening the chain and telling them to enjoy themselves, I made it back to my desk in time to catch another phone call on the fourth ring.

It went like that all morning, with fourteen people coming in and nine phone calls. I sold thirty-seven dollars worth of merchandise from the gift store, which I put into the cash box that was kept in Petra's desk. And it wasn't until after one o'clock in the afternoon that the onslaught ended. Then it was as quiet as it had been the week before. No phone calls and no visitors. It was like a five-hour stretch of the Twilight Zone. Or maybe the previous week had been the Twilight Zone, and now I was out of it. Although Petra had said it could be off and on like this.

It took me until almost two o'clock to finish all of Martha's typing. I sent it all off to Martha, took a deep breath, gazed longingly at the smooth movements of the fish in the tank behind me, and then I stood up to clear up the mystery of the boxes, upstairs and down.

Almost to the top of the stairs, I was thinking about the dilemma of the boxes, when I heard a sound behind me. I stopped on the stairs to listen, but it wasn't the bell, so it wasn't another customer. If it hadn't been for Rocky's tail hanging down from one of the top shelves in front of me, I'd have thought it might be him. That was curious, though, because usually he's so far hidden in those shelves that nobody can see him. The tail twitched. That was a mystery I'd have to solve another time. Carefully, I turned around on the steps and headed back down to discover what the sound was.

When I got to the bottom of the stairs, I wondered what were the possibilities of it being the murderer coming back to retrieve the rock or something. I looked around and didn't know what I could use as protection, so I walked into the bathroom and quietly grabbed the toilet plunger. It may not hurt him, but it might gross him out enough that I could get away. Holding the plunger over my head, I undid the chain to the back making sure it didn't make a sound. Then I slowly proceeded forward. And I found Aiden sitting on the floor, in the same spot I had found him before, holding a book on his lap.

He looked up when he saw me. "There're no toilets

back here, Lorry. The bathroom's behind you." He pointed behind me.

Embarrassed and without saying a word, I retraced my steps and put the plunger back in the bathroom, then returned to him. "What're ya doin', Aiden? Looking at pictures again?"

He glanced at the binder in front of him and looked up guiltily. "Um" was all he said.

I walked over to him. He was looking at the same "Taped Interviews" book as before. Turning a couple of pages, I saw there was a small picture of the person being interviewed, but otherwise, it was all text. "Aiden, you weren't looking at pictures, were you?"

Without looking up, he said, "No, Lorry."

"What were you doing then?"

He still wouldn't look at me. "Reading."

Reading. I thought about that. This was the kid who couldn't read. The kid who was in special ed classes because of his lack of reading skills. That made no sense. There was a problem somewhere. I had an inspiration. "Aiden, read that to me, will you?"

He nodded and began reading. "John Jonah Butler the second, aged seventy-eight, lived in Rutledge from 1895 to present. Interviewer: John, when did you move here? John Jonah Butler: Please call me Jonah. John is my father's name. Interviewer: All right, Jonah, when did you move here? John Jonah Butler: My family arrived here in 1895 from Pittsburg, Pennsylvania. We took a wagon train across some rough country back then, and boy were we ever happy to arrive safely when we reached Arizona."

The boy went on reading, and I stood there stupefied. He reads! He reads at an adult level! The kid shouldn't be in special ed, he should be in a class of gifted children. Aiden went on reading for several more minutes before I realized what I must do—and couldn't wait another minute to do so.

"Aiden, stop."

He looked up at me. "Did I miss a word?"

"No, Aiden, you didn't. Who taught you to read?"

"My Mommy—before she got all drugged up and went to heaven."

There wasn't a trace of anger in his voice, only remorse. He missed her. "So you're not reading at school because the baby books bore you, is that it?" He nodded. "Why don't you go to the school library and get a book that would interest you?"

"Because the librarian says my brothers and sisters should get their own books."

"You mean, she thinks the books you pick out are for your brothers and sisters?"

"Yes, that's right."

"What do you say me and you take a little trip to talk to your principal?"

He pushed the book away from him, and I could see the fright in his eyes. "I'm sorry! I won't do it anymore! Really! I can stop if I really want to!"

He can stop if he really wants to. In other words, he didn't *want* to stop reading. He *liked* reading. I ran over and threw my arms around him. "No, no, Aiden. You're not in trouble! I *want* you to read! I think it's *awesome* that you can read these advanced books. I want to take you to the principal to show her how well you read. And I want to take you to the library and get some books that will interest you. We'll go to the Rutledge Public Library instead of the school library. How about that?"

199

"Are you sure I won't get in trouble when they find out I can read?"

I nodded. "Yes, I'm sure. I *promise* you won't get in any trouble."

He pulled away and looked at me, tears sliding down his cheeks. "If you're sure, Lorry. Thank you."

The kid was breaking my heart. But now we had to go and face the principal.

CHAPTER FORTY-FOUR

I HEARD THE front door bell jingle, so I asked Aiden to stay there, and I walked to the front. It was Petra sans Mason.

"Hi, Lorry! The guy from Rutledge Taxi is going to call me today or tomorrow with the information."

"That's good. Listen, Petra. Can you hold down the fort? I have to take Aiden to the principal."

"*Why*? Did *Aiden* do something bad? I can't imagine *Aiden* doing anything bad."

"No. Aiden did something good. He did something really, really good." I looked up, and he was standing at the end of the hallway with a lopsided grin on his face.

"Lorry, you're *happy* that I can read? You think it's *good*?"

I ran over, grabbed him up, and hugged him to me as I walked back to Petra's desk. "I'm *very* happy you can read!"

He wiggled out of my arms and stood by Petra's desk. "Guess what, Petra? I can read!"

"That's really good, Aiden," she said while giving me a questioning glance.

"Petra," I said, "can I borrow one of your school books, please?" She unzipped her backpack, pulled out a book without looking, and handed it to me. I glanced at the cover, Psychology 101, and handed it to Aiden. "Read this, Aiden."

"He can't read that!" Petra reached out to take the book back, and I pushed her hand away.

"Yes, I can, Petra. Listen." And he began reading. "This book, Psychology 101, will take you from infant psychology to geriatric psychology, and everything in between. You will learn—"

"That's enough, Aiden." I tried to pull the book out of his hands, but he held on.

"It was just getting interesting, Lorry. I bet they have stuff in there about drugs. I'd like to read about drug addiction."

Petra sat there staring at Aiden with her mouth open. "He can read. I mean, he can *really* read."

"And Lorry is happy about it, so I'm going to continue," Aiden said with an upward tilt of his head that, if he was ten years older would be considered arrogant. But on a six-year-old, it looked cute.

"Come on, Aiden, let's go." I handed the book back to Petra, and Aiden and I walked toward the front door.

"I can't believe he can read. You give it to 'em, Lorry. This is unbelievable."

We walked along the side of the historical society building and toward the school. "I'm very proud of you, Aiden."

We were holding hands, but he grabbed me with his other hand and pulled himself off the ground in celebration. "Then I'm proud of me, too!"

When we approached the school, he became more

subdued. "Are you sure I won't get into trouble with the principal?"

"I am positive! I guarantee it! If anyone is going to get into trouble here, it *is* the principal!"

He giggled at this, and we walked into the school. The library straight ahead of us gave me an idea. We walked in and luckily the librarian was on break. No one was there. I pulled Aiden along to the children's section and picked out the easiest book I could find.

"I don't want that one, Lorry." He looked up at me, his eyes pleading.

I smiled at him. "Don't worry, Aiden. This book isn't for you, it's for the *principal!*" I think he understood, because he nodded his head emphatically and laughed.

As we left the library, Aiden pulled my hand. "Lorry, we have to check out the book. You can't just take it."

"We're *borrowing* it for five minutes, Aiden. It will be all right. Really."

He didn't seem convinced, but he came with me across the hall. Marylou was not in the office, and I was glad. Marylou, with her calming influence, would have taken the edge off. And I needed that edge to get my point across. I just hoped the principal was in her office. We walked out of the main office and a few steps to the left.

The door was partially closed. The nameplate said *Pamela Reilly, Principal*. We stood there while I gathered my courage. She wasn't on the phone, because I couldn't hear anything inside except the soft clicking of the computer keys. Aiden tugged on my sleeve and mouthed *"Are you sure?"* and I nodded, took a deep breath, knocked on the door and without waiting for a reply walked into the office pulling Aiden along with me.

CHAPTER FORTY-FIVE

"HELLO—" I HESITATED. Then I decided rather quickly that I would not address her as Mrs. Reilly, but I would take a more familiar tack. "Pamela. My name is Lorry Lockharte, and I think you know this guy."

"Hello, Mrs. Reilly," Aiden said with his head down.

"What can I do for you, Mrs. Lockharte?" She looked my age, dressed well but not extravagant, and had matching but sensible shoes on. And I hated when people assumed that I was married. Of course, when I *was* married, I didn't mind that assumption, so perhaps this was another attitude I needed to change.

"Lorry. Please call me Lorry." She nodded, and I continued. "I came to talk to you about Aiden's reading."

"Are you a relation of Aiden's that I didn't know about?"

To my surprise, Aiden grabbed my hand in both of his and looked up at me. "Lorry is my friend!"

I nodded. "As I said, I'm here about Aiden's reading. I'm his advocate."

Now, for the first time, she turned her chair to face me. "Aiden doesn't need an advocate. He is in special ed right now with our best reading teachers, and he gets supplementary reading assistance several times a week."

"He doesn't need any of that."

She smiled indulgently at me. "I'm sorry, Lorry, but you are not an educator, and you do not know what's good for the boy." She put her arms out for Aiden, but he pressed closer to me.

"No, I'm sorry, Pamela, but *you* don't know what's good for the boy." I handed her the children's book open to a random page. "Can you read this, please?"

Confused, she took the book and read "I hop, you hop, we all hop together." And then she looked up. "And what is your point, Lorry?"

"Read it again," I said innocently.

She read it again, and I asked her to read it again. She put the book down on her desk and looked at me, her eyes narrowed. "Come to the point, *Lorry!*"

"Is that book too boring for you, *Pamela?*"

"It's a beginning reader! Of course it's boring for me. But Aiden needs remedial reading, and this book *is* appropriate for *him!*"

I spotted a book on the other side of her desk called *Organics for Children.* Pointing to it, I asked her to pass it over. She looked at me questioningly, but I had been so audacious up to that point that she was probably a little afraid of what I might do if she refused. Then I handed the book to Aiden, put my hands on his shoulders, and looked into his eyes. "It's okay, Aiden. Show her what you can do, okay?"

"All right. Where should I start?" I flipped the pages to the introduction, and Aiden began to read. "There has always been controversy"—he hesitated briefly but sounded it out quickly and continued—"whether children in elementary school can benefit from organic fruits and vegetables. Will the sometimes exorbitant"— oh my goodness, I wasn't sure if *I* could pronounce exorbitant if someone put me on the spot like that —"costs of organic food prove cost-effective in terms of easier learning ability or higher intelligence quotients?"

When I glanced at Pamela Reilly, her mouth was hanging open even farther than Petra's had. And I was perfectly happy to shove her foot as far in as she could stand. But we had made our point. I returned the book to her desk.

She closed her mouth and looked at Aiden. Knowing better than to try to hug him with me standing guard, she reached out for one of his hands, and he reluctantly gave it to her. "I am so, so sorry, Aiden. I'm so sorry. Why didn't you say something earlier?"

I spoke up. "When he tried to get advanced books from the school librarian, she thought he was getting books for his brothers and sisters and wouldn't give them to him."

Pamela put her head on Aiden's hand in supplication. "I'm so sorry, Aiden. We didn't know." She glanced up quickly, and I saw tears at the corners of her eyes. I liked her a lot better after that. "Aiden, I promise you that we'll get you the books you need. Okay? We'll put you in an advanced reading class where you can read to your ability. Okay?"

Aiden looked up at me and I nodded. "Okay," he said softly.

Pamela stood up and reached out for my hand. She held it in both of hers. "Thank you so much, Lorry. You have done this child an incredible service."

"And you have done this child an incredible

disservice."

"I know that, and we will rectify that immediately. You can take my word on it."

Aiden looked up at me. "You were right, Lorry. I didn't get in any trouble."

I was curious about something. "Pamela, why is he so afraid of getting in trouble with the principal?"

"Oh, that. It's his older brother, who is in trouble all the time. He claimed that I hit him during detention one afternoon. But luckily my door was open and Marylou, who was right outside the office the entire time, confirmed that no such act occurred."

An idea occurred to me. "Aiden, did your brother tell you that if the school knew you could already read you'd get in trouble?" He nodded, and I hugged him and kissed him on the top of his head.

CHAPTER FORTY-SIX

AIDEN HANDED ME the library book we had borrowed and insisted that I return it. Then I left him with Pamela—who had an entirely different frame of mind than when I had arrived—and returned the book and walked back to the historical society. On the way there, I realized that Eddie had not been to see me in two whole days. Hopefully, he wouldn't show up anymore, but I realized that was too much to hope for. One thing was for sure, I could hardly wait until the divorce was final so I wouldn't have to deal with him anymore. Of course, I wasn't naive enough to believe that a simple divorce would stop Eddie from bothering me. He was like herpes: he may go away for a while, but sooner or later he'd return and make you miserable again.

When I walked to the front of the building, there was the red mustang again parked in front of the Koffee Korner. Had I wished him there by thinking about him? I slid into the door hoping he didn't see me.

"Hey, Petra. Eddie didn't turn up here, did he?"

"Haven't seen him. Say, Lorry, how did you figure out

that Aiden could read?"

"I caught him with one of those binders that had only a rare picture in it. He couldn't deny it. That reminds me, I want to finish my binder and box reconnaissance before I leave today."

"Too late, Lorry. Martha sent over some corrections to the papers you typed earlier today."

Ah-oh. "Corrections?" I asked, afraid to hear the answer. I was normally an incredibly accurate typist, but in my defense, it had been a busy morning.

"Oh, no, no. Nothing you had done. She needed to make corrections on her own work and now needs them changed. Too bad she can't type, huh?"

"If she could, maybe I wouldn't have a job." I walked into my office to find Martha's new folder on the desk, so I took the papers out and began the corrections.

"By the way, Lorry. The taxi guy never called. I am mucho disappointed."

"Mucho, huh?"

"Yeah. I know I'm right about Michael lying, but I just want it verified. Oh, and that reminds me, Martha said when you finish the typing, you can leave for the day. She appreciated the work you did around the house."

"Oh, all right."

I finished the work in twenty-seven minutes, bid my adieu to Petra, and drove home. But before I got out of the car, I realized that I had finished the casserole and there was nothing else to eat. So I drove to Rutledge Super Market and stocked up on more groceries, including butter and more cereal. Then I returned home to fix another batch of Noodle Knoodle. It was fast, it was easy, and I felt too tired to come up with anything else. A package of noodles, a pound of hamburger—

browned—a can of corn, a can of sliced olives, and tomato sauce were all the ingredients you needed. Plus, it was easy to remember. After cooking the noodles and browning the hamburger, I mixed it all together, put it in the oven, and thirty minutes later I was sitting at the table stuffing my face.

While I was at the store, I had picked up a *Rutledge Chronicle*. Although there was an online edition, it didn't always have all the ads in it—at least that's what I'd heard—and I didn't want to take any chances. Sometime if I had nothing better to do, I might check the paper copy with the online copy and see if that was true. It wouldn't be tonight. Martha and Hugo's house was comfortable, and right now I almost felt *obligated* to stay because of Hugo's hospitalization, but I would like my own place eventually.

And with the five thousand dollar check, I could cover first and last month's rent and get a decent place. And if the letter that came with the check was sincere about more financial assistance, then maybe sometime I could even buy my own house again. Wouldn't that be sweet?

And maybe, if that happened, I could realistically consider adopting Aiden. What a cute, sweet kid. I loved that kid. He had said his mother died from drugs, but he said nothing about his father. Maybe he didn't have a father—or at least didn't know who he was. I wondered how I could find out if he was even "adoptable," because I knew that some kids were, but other kids were stuck in the foster care program. I'd have to check that out, maybe the following day if it wasn't too busy.

CHAPTER FORTY-SEVEN

WHEN I WALKED into work in the morning, the phone was already ringing, and Petra was so involved in her computer work, that she was ignoring it. I rushed to answer it. "Rutledge Historical Society" was all I could get out before I ran out of breath. I needed to get some exercise. It was Pamela from Aiden's school, and she wanted to see me as soon as possible.

"Petra, can you cover for me for a short time? I need to go over to Aiden's school for something."

"Sorry, Lorry," she said as she hurried to the front door, "I have a test this morning. But it's perfectly fine to put up the sign and go out. Really. It's all right." She reached into the drawer, hung the sign on the door, and disappeared out the door.

Looking at the sign, which apparently Petra didn't do, I changed it from three P. M. to ten A. M. And I hoped that I would be back before then. Whatever could the school need *me* for? Surely Aiden didn't forget how to read overnight. I locked the front door and walked over to the school.

Marylou smiled at me when I walked into the office.

211

"Hi, Lorry! They're waiting for you in the teachers' lunchroom. 'Member where it is?"

"Sure! Thanks, Marylou!"

That confused me. I thought I was going to see Pamela. Who were *they*, I wondered as I walked up the stairs. The lunchroom's door was closed, so I knocked and not waiting for *them* to answer, I walked in.

"Hello, Lorry, come on in," Pamela said. I was already in, but why argue? "Lorry, I asked you here today so we could talk about Aiden's future."

Aiden's future, I wondered. What did *I* have to do with Aiden's future? This was confusing. "All right," I said cautiously.

"I'd like you to meet—" My head was spinning, and I couldn't concentrate on the names she said. I'd have to think of them as Tic and Tac. They looked alike anyway. I tried to focus as Pamela continued. "They are from the Arizona Department of Child Safety."

That frightened me. "Aiden is all right, isn't he?" I grabbed the back of a chair to steady myself. Dressed in dark suits, the two men looked mid-fifties and humorless. Tic and Tac fit them perfectly. They were the same height and weight and had the same attitude. Twins. They looked like TV cops or the FBI.

"Yes, yes, he's fine. We just want to talk to you, Lorry," said Tic.

"Sit down," said Tac.

"Mrs. Reilly told us what you discovered yesterday, and frankly it surprised us that no one else had realized that the boy could read in the months leading up to today. Why did the foster parents not discover this? They spend more time with the child than anyone."

It wasn't my job to stand up for an unknown foster

parent, but I felt like I needed to. "It's my understanding that she has nine other foster children." I shrugged. "Sounds like a lot of work."

"Yes, that explains it, but regardless, we would like to know if you would be interested in taking over foster care for this young boy. The hopefully *former* foster parents have reluctantly agreed, and we hoped you would take on this responsibility. The boy seems to like you."

I smiled. "And I like *the boy*. However, I'm not interested in being a foster parent." Calling Aiden *the boy* seemed demeaning, but I'd go along with it for now.

"Are you sure, Lorry? It could be beneficial to the boy, and I'm sure very gratifying to you as well."

"No, I'm sorry, I'm not interested in being his foster parent."

Both Tic and Tac had been talking, and I couldn't remember one from the other anyway, but when I said that, they both rose in unison, gathering up the papers in front of them. "I guess we're done here. Apparently you were wrong about her wanting the boy, Mrs. Reilly."

I waited a beat and then stood up to be on the same level with them. Smiling at them sweetly—they were much too business-like for a regular smile—I said, "Just a minute. *Pamela* was not wrong about me wanting Aiden. But I don't want to be a *foster* parent. I want to be a *real* parent. Can you tell me if he's adoptable?"

The men sat back down with two thumps, and I followed suit without the thump. "Lorry, adopting a child can be an overwhelming undertaking. It could be a thousand dollars or two. Can you afford that? Are you sure you don't want to become his foster parent, because being a foster parent pays *you* to take care of him. More than eight hundred dollars per month. Are you sure you wouldn't rather have that?" Tac asked.

Pamela cleared her throat and tried to say under her breath, "She's a Rutledge *Lockharte*."

The men must surely be from Coyote Moon and not Rutledge, but apparently they had heard of the Rutledge *Lockhartes*. People in town still called the old mansion that we used to live in so many years ago the *Lockharte* mansion. I saw both sets of eyebrows go up, but neither one said a word.

One or two thousand dollars. Where would I get that? Then I remembered about the financial assistance from the Rutledge *Lockhartes*. Plus, I still had the five thousand dollars. Yes, I could come up with the money. "No, I'm certain that I want to adopt him. No foster parenting."

Tic looked at me. "You would also have to complete a home study course before the adoption can go through."

What? Did he think I was uneducated? Who was it that discovered the kid could read? "I'm sure if I have trouble with it, Aiden can help me. You know, with the big words."

The two men looked at each other, but it was Pamela who cleared her throat again and spoke. "She's kidding, gentlemen." I think the throat clearing was to cover up an aborted laugh. I could learn to like that woman.

Tic and Tac stood up. Tac said, "I'll begin preparing the paperwork."

Yesterday, I couldn't even spell mother. And today, I *almost* are one.

CHAPTER FORTY-EIGHT

AS I CAME around the corner of the building, I checked my watch. Ten minutes after ten. Not bad. I was only ten minutes late from what I had put on the sign. Stepping up to the building, I unlocked the door. I had my hand on the handle ready to open it, when I noticed handsome Ezra Yoke walking out of the Koffee Korner Kafe, so I smiled in greeting. But he wasn't smiling. I opened the door and walked in, leaving the door open behind me for Ezra. Whatever was going on with him made me uncomfortable. He was rapidly falling from my number one crush to a distant number two.

He came through the door and closed it none too quietly. Not a slam, but not a quiet closure, either. "Lorry!" he said accusingly. "This business should be open at nine o'clock! What is the meaning of this?" Ezra grabbed the *Be Right Back!* sign and tossed it onto my desk. "What kind of way is *that* to run a business?"

I opened my mouth to speak, but his *attack* dumbfounded me so much that nothing came out. He glared down at me with his blue eyes blazing. Fortunately, I was saved by the bell. The phone bell, that is. The phone rang. In the position I was in, I could have picked the phone up without moving. Instead, I turned my chair completely around so that I faced the computer, and then I answered the phone with my back to Ezra.

In a word, I was dismissing him. I didn't deserve that kind of abuse—I had enough of it with Eddie—and I wasn't going to take it anymore. The call was only a basic inquiry about the historical society, but I kept the phone in my hand answering imaginary questions until he walked away. When I heard him walking up the stairs, I said goodbye—I don't like to hang up without a goodbye even if the conversation is imaginary—and then hung up the phone.

A minute later, after I had locked my purse in the drawer and turned on the computer, a courier appeared at the door. It was the fifteen-year-old boy who Martha sends over with her paperwork. With a shy smile, he handed me a yellow manila folder filled with papers and stepped back out the door.

The paperwork consisted of several new documents, so I started typing. I could hear Ezra upstairs moving boxes around. When I was up there, it appeared that nothing had been done. I wondered exactly *what* he had been helping Betty with. Maybe I should have asked more questions when he first asked to help. Although, except when he got in his *moods*—like today—I liked having him around. Shaking my head, I forgot about it and proceeded with the typing.

It felt like hours later before I sat back and took a breath. Someone else must have written some of the documents, because they weren't Martha's broad handwriting and instead were a tiny script that I had to keep holding up to my face to interpret. It wasn't just tiny writing that was the problem, it was nearly illegible.

When I looked at the clock on the computer, it was already one o'clock. I kept typing. In the background, I heard Ezra use the bathroom once, but besides one phone call about the hours of the historical society and if we were open on the weekends, it was quiet. Then Martha called at two-thirty asking me to send the files I had already finished. She said she wasn't rushing me but only wanted the ones that were finished. I was facing the computer and had just pushed send on the email when I heard the bell announce the door was opening.

I looked up so I could greet whoever was coming in with a smile when I realized the *whoever* was Eddie. My smile drooped. He hadn't bothered me for a couple of days, and I had begun to think he wouldn't come back. Think again, Lorry, I told myself. "Oh, it's you."

"You're not glad to see me?" Eddie asked. He wore black slacks with a sharp crease on the legs, a black shirt, black tie, and black shoes. They were all new. And I still wore the same old clothes I had when I was married to him.

"Are you trying to imitate Johnny Cash? You'd never have his style."

With one hand flared down and one hand flared up like a model, he said, "Yes, but I'm better looking."

"Says who?"

He unflared his hands and pointed a finger at me. "Look. You just got a check for five thousand dollars. I want half of it. You're still married to me."

I raised a finger to him and waved it back and forth. "I've already filed for divorce. So I don't think that counts."

"I don't care if it counts or not, I want the money."

"And I don't care if it counts or not, either. You're not getting a dime! Now get out of my life and leave me alone." Turning my back on him, I faced the computer.

He stepped forward, grabbed my shoulder—hard—and spun me around to face him. "I said I want it!"

"Ouch, Eddie, get your filthy paws off me!"

And at that moment, like my personal savior from heaven, handsome Ezra Yoke came racing down the stairs to confront Eddie. In that second that I heard his footsteps, I completely forgave all his moods and was once again under the spell of his charms.

"Hey!" he yelled from the other end of the hall. He wasn't the kind of guy who would run up to Eddie.

Eddie stepped back, and I saw fear on his face. By that time, Ezra stood right in front of him, close enough to smell Eddie's bad breath. And he looked down at him like he was a turd that he had accidentally stepped on. "What are you doing to Lorry?" Ezra punched him in the chest with his finger. Several times.

Eddie stepped back again and said, "She owes me money!"

Ezra glanced at me, and I shook my head no. "And *what* does she owe you money for?" His voice wasn't raised, but it had the tone of someone reprimanding a recalcitrant five-year-old. And that was a good description of Eddie.

"She's my wife! She received a check, and I want half of it."

Ezra shook his head and looked confused. "I could have sworn I heard her say that she had filed for divorce. Didn't you say that, Lorry?" He looked at me, and I nodded. "That eliminates you right there as her husband, doesn't it? Now what do you really want that money for?" With his finger, he poked Eddie in the chest again. "Drugs, right?"

I think Eddie would have been livid if he hadn't been so scared, so he said, "*I* don't do drugs!" He liked to act like he was tough, but he was a wimp.

That was one thing about Eddie, he may have been a piece of garbage, but he was telling the truth, he never did do drugs—at least since he had been with me. Before that, I'm not sure. He probably smoked a little pot in high school. So when Ezra glanced my way, I shook my head.

Ezra narrowed his eyes and looked at Eddie. "Hmmm. No drugs, huh? Let's see, what else could a piece of garbage like you be into?" He put his hand to his temple like he was thinking. "Aha! I got it! You want the money for gambling!"

Eddie turned a bright red and glared at me. I held up my hands like I hadn't said anything—and I hadn't—at least not to Ezra. Well, not to anybody, because everyone I knew *already* knew Eddie was a degenerate gambler.

"So you want the money for gambling. Too bad!"

Then Eddie stood up on his tiptoes—I'm not exaggerating, he really did that—and tried to look Ezra in the eyes, but even on his tiptoes, he wasn't tall enough. "She took money out of our joint account when she left me! And I want it back!"

Ezra didn't have to look at me that time, because I laughed right out loud. "Eddie, you are still the dirty liar you've always been! *You* are the one who completely emptied our joint account before we took the trip to the Grand Canyon, and I didn't even know about it until I got home! If anything, *you* owe *me* money!"

Ezra took his hand, put it on top of Eddie's head, and

pushed, so Eddie had to come off his tiptoes. Then he leaned over and put his face close to Eddie's again. "I think *you*"—he hesitated—"owe the lady some money, big shot. Now give it to her."

Eddie quickly turned around and put his hand on the doorknob, but Ezra was quicker. He reached over Eddie's head and held the door closed. Eddie frantically looked for somewhere else to run to, but he was trapped. The glassed-in gift shop was behind him, the door was held closed, and Ezra stood in front of him. You could see his whole bearing sink into the floor.

"I said, give her the money," Ezra repeated.

"I'm calling the police as soon as I leave here," said Eddie.

"Besides poking you in the chest, *after* you assaulted my friend, Lorry, what else did I do to you? Absolutely nothing, that's what. Now give her the money."

"I didn't assault her!"

"Lorry, did he hurt you?"

"Yes! He grabbed my shoulder, and it hurt!"

"You better give her the money, little man, or I will insist that you give her your clothes as well."

Eddie looked up at Ezra disbelieving, but then decided that he might mean it. He didn't want to lose his new gangsta-looking outfit. Slowly, he reached into his wallet, pulled out two fives, three ones, and a ten, and handed them to me.

Ezra, watching the exchange, nodded his head. "That's a good start, little man, now give her the rest."

"I need something to live on!"

"You didn't leave Lorry anything to live on when you emptied the bank account, did you? Okay, I warned you. Take off your shoes."

"What?"

"I said give her the rest *and* take off your shoes."

Eddie reached into his wallet, withdrew three hundred dollar bills and a fifty, and threw them at me. They floated down onto the desk. "There! That's all I have!"

"And now your shoes," said Ezra in a soft, soothing voice. "You will take off your shoes or you will not leave here." He reached above Eddie and put his hand back on the door.

"I can't believe this!"

"Do it!" said Ezra in a loud, commanding voice.

When Eddie slipped off his shoes and kicked them over to me, Ezra stepped back. As Eddie stomped out the door—as much as you can stomp in your stockinged feet —Ezra called out, "I don't *ever* want to see you bothering Lorry again! And I mean *never!*"

CHAPTER FORTY-NINE

IN SILENCE, EZRA and I watched Eddie hobble by the front window. When he disappeared from view, I couldn't help myself. I jumped up and threw myself into Ezra's arms. "Thank you so much! That was awesome! I can't believe Eddie gave me that money! He's never given me a dime before!"

"Well, it's about time, Lorry." Then he released me from his arms and looked at me. I thought he would kiss me, I *hoped* he would kiss me, but he didn't. Color me disappointed. Then he said, "Lorry, why would a lovely woman like yourself ever team up with a piece of garbage like that? I don't understand."

"Believe me, Ezra, I've been asking myself the same question—for years." Then I got inspired. "Listen, Ezra, you just saved me from the aforementioned piece of garbage. And you got me all this money!" Picking up two of the hundreds, I waved them in the air. "What a windfall! How about if I take you to dinner tonight to celebrate?"

He didn't answer. He glanced quickly at his watch and said, "Oh! I need to get out of here. I left something upstairs. Be right back."

I heard him run up the stairs. Petra came through the door then. Ezra came down quickly and rushed down the hallway almost running into Petra. He said nothing, just pushed past her, and walked out.

Petra looked at me, puzzled. "What was *he* doing up there?"

Sometimes she could be such a teenager! What was wrong with that girl? It was such a stupid question that I didn't even give her an answer. I turned back to the computer to finish the final document. Of course she knew what he was doing here. He had been helping Betty.

Several minutes later, I finished the document, attached it to an email, and sent it off. Now maybe I could get a chance to finish investigating the boxes. Still peeved at Petra for being such a stinker, I just walked past her, ignoring her. But she didn't realize that I was ignoring her, because she was faced toward her computer and didn't even know that I walked by. I hated it when that happened. It takes a lot of oomph to ignore someone, and for that person to ignore your ignoring is plain frustrating.

I hiked up the stairs and then walked over to the boxes on the floor and the binders on the shelves to refresh my memory. The binders starting with A and C were already on the shelves. The rest of the boxes on the floor were in *alphabetical order*. So Betty had been putting them away *alphabetically*. The end box—the last one brought up before her *accident*—the one that I had noticed before was "People." And the box that Betty allegedly dropped as she met her death was a box labeled "Timeline." "Timeline" did not come directly after "People." Now I had to re-check the downstairs boxes, so I raced down the stairs holding onto the rail so I wouldn't meet *my* death.

When I arrived at the boxes closest to the back door and *farthest* from the stairs, the end box was "Police Beat." "Police Beat" would be the one that would come after "People." *Not* "Timeline." It all came clear. Betty didn't try to carry that box upstairs. The killer had arranged it to look like that. This was the proof I needed to show that *both* sisters had been murdered.

I stood there, staring at the Police Beat binders and congratulating myself when I heard the bell on the door ring. Even from the back, I could hear Petra on the phone, so I walked briskly to the front. It was Michael Wellesley. I smiled at him. Now that I knew he couldn't have been the killer, I felt sorry for him losing both his sisters like that.

Before I got to where Petra could see me, she hung up the phone with a bang, and shouted out, "Lorry! I was right! Michael was lying! The taxi guy said he got to town the evening *before* the murder!"

Michael Wellesley looked stricken. He grabbed for my desk to stay upright.

"Um, Petra." I stopped at her desk, leaving Michael on his own to hold himself up. "Two things. One is that Michael is standing in my office listening to your every word. The second is that I just discovered evidence that clears him. His sister Betty was murdered, too. And it had to have been the same murderer."

Petra nodded her head and then jumped up and ran to Michael Wellesley. "I'm so sorry, Michael, I'm so sorry." She put her hand on his arm, but he had his head down covered with both hands.

I walked in and put my hand on his other arm and gave it a little squeeze. "I'm sorry, Michael. We've been trying to solve Gwen's murder, and you have been the only suspect."

"What about that kid who's in jail?"

"I knew he didn't do it," said Petra.

"He was in jail when Betty was murdered," I said.

He looked up with tears streaming down his face. "And you thought *I* had done it? That I had killed both my sisters?" He looked down again, and the tears started anew. "I lied because I was with a woman that night," he said without looking up. "A married woman!"

Both of us were stroking his arms and trying to make him feel better, but it wasn't working. Finally, with one hand still covering his eyes, he pulled away from us. "I need to get out of here." Without another word and without looking up, he opened the door and slipped outside.

"Wow." Petra looked out the window at Michael walking down the street. "I messed up, didn't I?"

"It could have been worse, Petra—but I can't imagine how."

She nodded her head. "Yeah."

Sitting down at the desk, I reached for the phone. "I need to call Billy to tell him what I found."

Petra quickly stepped over, grabbed the phone, and slammed it down. "You can't! He's got a date tonight."

225

CHAPTER FIFTY

I'D LIKE TO say that I didn't care that Billy had a date. After all, I had just melted into Ezra's arms. But the truth was, it bothered me. Jealous? How could I be jealous? I wasn't an expert on the machinations of jealousy, but I was pretty sure that's what I was feeling. Plus, I thought it was important that he find out this information as soon as possible. At least, that's what I told myself.

"Petra, as soon as he finds this out, it will mean your friend Zack can go free."

"It won't hurt Zack to spend one more night in jail. Billy hasn't had a date in ages, and he needs this."

"Petra, you're not being logical. This is a *murder* investigation! He needs to know!" I reached for the phone again, and she pushed it back down in its cradle.

"No, Lorry. This is important to me. Now I want you to promise me that you won't call him." She continued to hold the phone down.

I crossed my arms over my chest. "No, I refuse to promise! This is important and some things are more important than other things. Murder is more important than his *date!*"

Petra stepped back and a smile crossed her face. "I do believe you're jealous."

"I am not!" I protested.

She laughed. "Yes, you are, and you're not leaving here until you promise me you will not call him."

I kept my arms across my chest. And although I pretended to resist the promise, it occurred to me that I had found a little loophole. But I didn't intend to let her guess how I'd utilize said loophole. "All right!" I said in a raised voice. "I promise I won't call him!"

Petra laughed again. "That's better. You're welcome to go home now. It's nearly five. I'll hold down the fort. Although I'm leaving early today—I have a big test tomorrow, and I need to study."

I fished the key out of the back of the top drawer, opened the bottom drawer, and extracted my purse. Then I turned off the computer, picked up Eddie's shoes, and without even a hint of a smile, walked past Petra who was diligently working on a spreadsheet on her computer, and I huffed out, "Goodbye!" in a fake angry voice. I hoped that she wouldn't realize it was fake. As I walked down the back hallway, I had to bite my lip to keep from giggling, because I got one past her. I justified what I was about to do by virtue of the fact that she could have made me promise not to *contact* him, but that's not what she did. I just took advantage of her lack of clarity, and I wasn't going to feel guilty about that.

Outside, after I made sure the door was locked, I dropped Eddie's shoes into the dumpster. Then I jumped into my car and started it. Giggling to myself, I knew I had to drive away before Petra figured out my loophole. Off I drove toward Main Street and the Sheriff's Office.

But I didn't lie. I had said I wouldn't *call* him. Never had I said *anything* about not going to *see* him.

Taking the alley to Bridge Street, I turned right, and then right again on Main. I parked in the parking lot and looked at the white concrete building. This was the third time in a week I'd been there. I'd be glad when this murder case was solved, so I could go back to my *normal* life.

Although, my *previous* normal life was anything but normal. Being married to Eddie—to an inveterate gambler—mimicked the highs and lows of his gambling. When he won, things were great. He'd bring me gifts— never any money, of course, but gifts—and we'd go out to expensive dinners. And when he lost, it was like the whole world was coming to an end. Life couldn't have gotten any worse—for him or for me. Grateful that was not my life anymore, I treaded toward the door, still a little pleased with myself for getting one over on Petra.

I used both hands to pull open the heavy door, and I stepped inside. The buzzer went off again, announcing my presence. The same Civilian Officer as before came to the window.

"Hi, again. Is Sheriff Billy here? I really need to talk to him."

"Yes, he hasn't left yet. I'll tell him you're here." She spoke softly on a phone and then said, "He'll be right here."

"Thanks so much."

A minute later Billy stepped out the door with a big smile on his face. "Lorry! To what do I owe this honor?" He reached out and put his hand on my shoulder. Billy was a cuddly kind of guy.

"I found new evidence, Billy. For real."

His smile evaporated. "Really? Tell me."

While I explained about the boxes, he nodded in understanding with a serious look on his face. I concluded with "Billy, you really need to see what I'm talking about. I can't do it justice with words."

He gave a sharp nod. "Yes, you're right. Let's go."

"You believe me?" It surprised me that he had listened to my story and was so willing to go along with it.

He looked at me and furrowed his brows. "Of course I believe you, Lorry. *You* are the one who found the murder weapon! And by the way, it *was* Gwen's blood. The DNA matched."

Raising my eyebrows at the new information, I nodded and said, "Yeah, you're right. I did." I looked at my watch. "Um, do you think we can wait a few more minutes?"

"Why?"

"Because I promised Petra I wouldn't call you."

"Whyever not?"

This was all so stupid, I felt embarrassed to tell him. I looked at the ceiling so I wouldn't have to look in his eyes. It wasn't only the embarrassment—I didn't want him to see the jealousy there. "Because she said you had a date, and she didn't want me to disturb you."

Billy burst out laughing. "While I appreciate Petra looking out for my welfare, a murder investigation *does* have priority over a date." My stomach lurched until he continued. "And it isn't a *date*, anyway! I'm going to dinner with an old high school friend—yes, a female— *and*, her husband."

I laughed and tried to hide my relief.

CHAPTER FIFTY-ONE

I PARKED IN the back, and Billy pulled the patrol car into the slot next to mine. Trying to slip the key in the lock and turn it silently—hoping that Petra had already left—I couldn't get it to open. When I tried again, it opened right away. Petra or no Petra, we were going in.

Billy held the door open for me, and I walked in first. "Petra? Petra?" No answer. Thank goodness. I would deal with that fallout tomorrow, but since Billy didn't have a date anyway, it didn't matter too much.

"All right. Here are some of the boxes, but it would be easier to explain if we went upstairs first."

"Yeah, sure. Lead the way."

We walked upstairs, and when we got to the top, Rocky meowed and I sneezed. We both looked up to see Rocky stretching and doing a downward dog—you know, a yoga pose—and then Billy opened his arms, and Rocky jumped right into them. Then Billy kissed the top of Rocky's head, while Rocky rubbed against him.

Although I'm not fond of cats—can't stand 'em, really—it made me like Billy a little more than I already did. A man who likes animals is a good man. He was rapidly gaining ground on smooth, suave Ezra, especially after I had asked Ezra to dinner and he ran out on me without even answering. But then, what frightened me a little was that Petra had told me Rocky only did that with her. Was I in danger of being *cat attacked?* I hoped not.

Billy put Rocky back on the shelf from where he had jumped, and then he looked at me. "All right. Show me."

"Come over here." I led him over to where the boxes were on the floor and the binders were on the bookshelf. "See the binders? A's and C's . . . the beginning of the alphabet. And see the boxes on the floor are alphabetical, as well. The last boxes are some of the P's. See, these binders are all labeled People." The binders inside the box were slightly askew. Ezra must have been looking through them. I thought he was helping Betty with something, and yet, besides the binders being moved, no work had been done. None at all. Hmmmm. Not for me to think about right now. "Now let's go back downstairs."

When we walked past the bookshelves by the stairs, Rocky stood up again and moved like he was going to jump, but Billy held up his hand. "Not now, Rocky. Not now." At least the cat listened. That was one thing in his favor.

We descended the stairs, and I took Billy toward the boxes closest to the back door. "See? The next one that should have gone upstairs would have been Police Beat, but instead, the box that Betty supposedly dropped was"—I walked over to the box closest to the chain —"Timeline. Betty was doing everything *alphabetically*. She wouldn't have moved everything up there in order and suddenly one out of order. Although I didn't know her, from what I can see of what she'd already done, I know she wouldn't do that."

Billy looked pensive. He walked by the boxes again, nodding his head, then he ran up the stairs and came back down again a minute later. "You're absolutely right, Lorry. She wouldn't have done that." Then he ran up the stairs again.

This time I followed. At the top of the stairs, he picked Rocky up and put him on the floor. Rocky moved back and forth across Billy's legs. I sneezed and rubbed my eyes. Billy began pushing the books back in the bookshelf, and after watching him do it, I realized what he was doing. He was looking to see if there was *another* murder weapon up here. A second later, he found it. Pulling the books from the shelf, he peered over the edge, looked in, and nodded his head. "You can't see this high up, Lorry, but there it is." He turned toward me and put out his arms like he was going to grab me and pick me up. When I stepped back with my hands in the *no closer* position, he thought better of it. "Another quartz crystal, just like before. I can't see blood on it, but I'm sure it's there." Then he keyed his mike and called for the forensic team.

"They'll be here in a few minutes. You don't need to stay. It won't take long, and I'll lock up when they're finished." He gave me a broad smile. "You can trust me!"

Billy was a handsome man. He didn't have the sophistication that Ezra had, but he had a certain earthiness that I liked. It was different from Eddie and his phoniness. Much different. I liked it, and I smiled at him. When I turned to go, he gently grabbed my arm.

"Lorry, you've done great work on this. Really. I'm sorry I doubted you before."

232

I turned back toward him and tilted my head. "You realize, Billy, two of the same murder weapons, same *MO*, it has to be the same murderer, don't you think? Which means that Zack is innocent."

"MO, huh? Are you thinking I should make you a deputy or something?" We both laughed at that. "I'll have paperwork to do, but yes, it would be unlikely that two murderers would have the same *MO* like this. Zack will be out by tomorrow. And again, good call, Lorry." Then he looked at me seriously and put his hand on my shoulder, too firmly for a friendly pat. "This guy is dangerous. He's killed two people. You need to leave it to us now and let me do the investigating. I don't want you getting hurt. All right?"

"My work is done!" I said, but at the same time I wondered who would do such a thing and why. If I found out the why, that might tell me the *who*. I waved goodbye to Billy, still thinking of the possibilities.

CHAPTER FIFTY-TWO

ON MY WAY home, I stopped at the convenience store on the corner of Commercial and Bridge, to pick up a newspaper. If I was going to adopt Aiden, and it looked like I was, I needed another place to live. A place we could call our own.

When I pulled in front of Martha and Hugo's house, I saw her car in the driveway. I wondered if Hugo was home. But when I walked into the house, she had more clothes laid out on the couch ready to take with her back to the hospital. It disappointed me. The big house was lonely without Martha and Hugo there.

"Hi, Lorry!" Martha came out of the kitchen with a big smile on her face. "I'm so glad I ran into you! Thank you so much for cooking that delicious casserole! I can't get enough of it! You'll have to give me the recipe."

"Sure, Martha." She was always so ebullient and complimentary. Sad to say, I wasn't used to that. "It's easy to make and tastes great, so it's always my go-to recipe. How's Hugo?"

"Doctors say he's progressing really well, and if he continues in that direction, he can come home next

Monday. I'm grateful that he's okay. It could have gone either way." She gathered her belongings together and then looked at me again. "Lorry, I heard that you taught Aiden to read! That's so great!"

"No, Martha, I didn't teach him to read. I *discovered* that he could already read. At an adult level! He's a pretty amazing kid." Then I thought I may as well tell her. It would be common knowledge soon in the town anyway. "And I've put in to adopt him. They're working on the paperwork now."

Martha covered the few steps between us in a heartbeat and threw her arms around me. "Oh, Lorry! I am so happy to hear that! I think you'll make a great mother. You're welcome to stay here if you want."

"You mean *with* Aiden?"

"Yes, of course with Aiden. I think having a child in the house again will do Hugo good. It will help him heal."

Holding out the newspaper to her, I said, "I just got this to try and find a place to live. Now I can take my time and be a little pickier. Thank you!"

"Oh, don't go moving off so quickly. We'd love to have you stay here. Honestly."

I smiled at her. "Thank you so much, Martha. I appreciate that."

"Gotta run now, Lorry. Bye!" And she rushed out the door.

As I ate my warmed up casserole, I had the want ads in front of me, but there were no decent rentals available. Decent being the salient word. Even in Rutledge, there was a poor side of town. And although I knew that I shouldn't, I couldn't help myself. I let my eyes wander to the sales. It was a mistake. There was a cute, little house a few blocks from here in an upscale neighborhood. I'd have to look online to get any decent photos of it, but the way the text described it, it sounded perfect for Aiden and me. I sighed and closed the paper. No use torturing myself.

After cleaning up the kitchen, I walked upstairs. It had been an emotional day. First offering to adopt Aiden, and then, even before the shouting was over, a confrontation with Eddie, a rejection from Ezra, and then discovering the clue that led Sheriff Billy to the second murder weapon. All I wanted was to lie down on my bed and drift off to sleep not thinking about anything. Instead, I decided to torture myself some more.

While my computer started up, I changed into my nightgown and robe. I was serious about drifting off to sleep, but I had to do one thing first. I wanted to look up that cute, little house and see if there were any pictures posted online. Then I plugged my cell phone in to charge it. Even if nobody called, the thing still lost its juice. Nothing's perfect. I keyed in Realtor.com and looked for the house. A few clicks and there it was.

It was a small gambrel house—the kind that looks like a barn. It was even painted red with white trim, and it was darling. A shade tree out front complimented the well-kept yard. Aiden would like to climb that tree. I hope he's careful! A picture of the backyard showed a swing set. I wondered if they would want to sell that. The inside looked homey, with a wood stove in the living room, an eating bar between the kitchen and living room, and two large bedrooms with a smaller one used as an office. The bigger bedroom had its own bathroom —that would be mine. The other bedroom had plenty of room for Aiden and all his toys. And books. Since the kid loved to read, I'd have to buy him plenty of books. Fantasy, fantasy, fantasy. Wishful thinking. Magical thinking. Idiotic thinking. Wait. Before I disparaged myself any further, let's take a look at this. I wanted to adopt this kid and now I'm going to. That wasn't wishful thinking or idiotic thinking, I wanted it, and I made it happen. Maybe the house wasn't out of my reach after all.

CHAPTER FIFTY-THREE

THE FOLLOWING MORNING before going to work, I drove by the gambrel house. It made me sigh. It was even cooler than the pictures showed. The street was tree-lined, and a canopy of trees shaded almost the whole yard. That was good for a hot Arizona summer. I shook my head. It was so perfect. And then I saw it. A bicycle leaning against the rail. A boy's bike. A boy the size of Aiden. It made me smile. I felt like it was a sign that I would somehow get the house.

When I arrived at the historical society, Petra was already there. She was deep into her spreadsheet as I walked by. "Lorry, there's a note for you on your desk." She clicked away at the keyboard. "Can you wait just a minute until I finish the column?" A few clicks later, she turned to me with a big smile on her face. "You're adopting Aiden? That's so cool! How did that happen?"

"If you know that, you should know how it happened."

"Lorry! Don't be snotty. I know because the message on your desk is to pick up the adoption papers at the school. And Aiden is the only kid you know. So how did it happen?"

After I apologized to Petra, I explained how I had given the principal the riot act, and how she had recommended me to become a foster parent. And on and on, and I finished by saying, "I couldn't be happier. He is the greatest kid."

"How soon is it going to happen?"

"I don't know. Soon, I hope. I'll find out after I fill out the paperwork, I guess. I have to do a home study course, too, though."

Petra frowned. "You know, Lorry, I don't know much about it, but a friend of mine's mother adopted a kid, and it took months before it happened."

"Really?" Color me disappointed again. I would have been happy bringing Aiden home right away. "I'll get more details when I pick up the paperwork."

"And, hey! You broke your word! I saw fingerprinting dust all over the stairs and that box closest to the chain. You said you wouldn't call Billy!" She crossed her arms in front of her chest and then continued. "Lie. An untruth. False statement made to deceive."

"You're not talking to that lying scamp of an ex-husband of mine, young lady. I *do not* lie, and I did not *call* Billy."

"I didn't think you would lie, that's why I was surprised at the mess in here this morning. How did he find out, then?"

I shrugged and looked away. "I went to *see* him. You didn't say I couldn't do that!"

"You little sneak!" Petra said, and we both laughed. "What about his date?"

"It wasn't a date, Petra. He was going to dinner with a female friend from high school *and* her husband."

"Oh, I guess you have nothing to worry about then." She winked at me, but I didn't react to her teasing.

Walking over to my desk, I picked up the note that Petra had written. Pamela wanted to see me at the school at nine-thirty. I still had some time. It would take less than five minutes to walk over to the school. So I turned around and walked past Petra. "I'm going to go look at the damage upstairs."

"It's downstairs, too. You don't have to clean it. Martha will get someone in here."

"I don't mind." The box closest to the chain was covered in fingerprint dust as well as every binder inside the box. It was a mess. Then I walked upstairs as Rocky was walking downstairs. "Hello, mister," I said as I sneezed. He had fingerprint dust all over him. At the top of the stairs, there weren't as many quartz rocks—er, crystals—as downstairs, but every one was covered with the dust. The shelves had a heavy coat of the stuff, too. "This is awful, Petra! Maybe I'll rescind my cleaning offer!"

Petra said something, but I couldn't hear her. I looked again at the boxes of binders on the floor and the binders on the shelf. It had been exactly this way from the first time I saw this room. What had Ezra been doing up here? Besides the binders in the People boxes looking disturbed, nothing had been done—certainly not anything that Betty would need help with. That was curious.

I returned downstairs and stopped again at Petra's desk. She was trying to get the fingerprint dust off Rocky's silky fur. Since I had never petted the cat, I didn't know for sure his fur was silky, but it looked that way. I sneezed again and rubbed my nose.

240

"You know, you can take something for that. Some homeopathy thing or something."

"What's homeopathy?"

"Forget it. I'll find you some and bring it to you."

"Petra? Something occurred to me. Remember yesterday when you saw Ezra Yoke?"

"Who?"

"The tall, older man with graying hair and the suit? The suave, sophisticated one? You asked what he was doing upstairs. Why did you ask that?"

"Because he and Betty had a big argument. I thought she kicked him out."

"You're kidding. He told me that he was helping Betty with something."

"Well, *that's* not true. I'm sure of it."

I looked at my watch and realized that I'd have to hurry to the school. "Well, I'll have to think about that one. But I have to leave now. Would you mind putting the sign up before you leave?"

"'Course not. See ya later."

CHAPTER FIFTY-FOUR

THE MEETING WITH Pamela went well but was disappointing. She suggested that since it might take months for the adoption to go through that I should become Aiden's foster parent first. Of course, that, too, had its issues. I had to take several classes and go through all kinds of rigmarole. When I asked her if I could take him home that night, she thought I was joking. I laughed, too, but I wasn't joking. The sooner the better. What a great kid, and how lucky I was to be able to adopt him.

As I walked back to the historical society, I wondered if Ezra would be waiting at the door again. Angry again. And then I wondered what he had been doing upstairs, and why he had lied about helping Betty. When I walked around the corner, it wasn't Ezra pounding on the door and squinting into the room, it was Michael Wellesley.

I rushed up to him. "Michael? Is everything all right?"

"Oh! Hi! I thought you should see this!"

He handed me a piece of paper, but instead of looking at it, I unlocked the door so we could go inside. After putting my purse on my chair, I looked at the piece of paper. Although I didn't understand it—*H. H. Holmes* —> *Ezra Yoke*—all the blood drained from my face. Because I didn't think it could mean anything good. "What do you think it means?"

"I googled it! H. H. Holmes is the serial killer from the 1893 Chicago World's Fair!"

I shook my head, still not comprehending. "I still don't get it. Does this note mean that Ezra is a serial killer?"

"Well, I'm not sure. But Yoke is the last name of *one* of the spouses of H. H. Holmes—although he was still married to his first wife at the time. He was a bigamist several times over. But if Ezra Yoke is a relative of *that spouse*, that would mean that Georgiana Yoke was pregnant when Holmes was hanged."

My mind was now working overtime. Ezra had been upstairs for days "helping" while getting nothing done. Could one of his relatives have lived in Rutledge before, and he was trying to erase the connection between them? A cold chill ran through me from my head to my toes. All this time I thought he was suave and sophisticated, and he might be the killer! "Michael, I've got to go check something! Thank you for this!" I handed him back the paper and raced into the back.

I was up two stairs before I stopped to think. Ezra had probably been going through the People binders for all the days he'd been here, and he had found nothing. So maybe it was still downstairs. Walking back and forth in front of the boxes of binders, I looked at the labels. Which would be the most likely to contain what he was looking for? *I* didn't even know what he was looking for, but I had to use my imagination.

Timeline? Probably not. Taped Interviews? I didn't think so. Streets and Roads? Definitely no. Schools? No.

Rutledge Chamber of Commerce? No. Parades? No. Police Beat? Yeah, that could be the one. There were binders underneath the top binders that could have been different, but I'd start with Police Beat. If a relative of Ezra's had done something bad that Ezra wanted to hide, then that would be a good place to begin looking.

I sat down on the floor by the first box of binders and started to skim. A half hour went by, and I had come up with nothing. Then the back door opened. At this point, I didn't know what to expect. If Ezra was the killer, he could come in here any second, find me with the binders, realize that I had found him out, and kill me like he had killed Betty and Gwen. So when the door closed and Aiden walked toward me, I felt greatly relieved.

"What are you doing here, little one? You have books to read at school now, don't you? Books that you like?"

He nodded. "I just wanted to come see you." He dropped down to the floor sitting right in front of me. "Someone at school said you were going to be my new mommy, and I wanted to ask you for myself. Things I hear at school aren't always the truth, so I wanted to come to the source and hear it from you."

Come to the source. This kid will entertain me my entire life. What a charmer. As agitated as I was, he still made me smile. That made me shove the Police Beat binder to the side and open my arms for him. He climbed right into my lap, and I closed my arms around him. "Aiden, I'm going to adopt you. Is that all right with you?"

"Yeah! I'd love for you to be my mommy!" He looked up at me with those deep blue eyes of his and smiled. "Can I come home with you tonight?"

He wasn't even officially mine, yet, and we were already thinking alike. "No, sweetie, it will take a little while, but we'll be together soon. Okay?" Aiden nodded, and I continued. "Why don't you go back to school now? I can walk you there." I knew I shouldn't let him go by himself, but he didn't have to cross any streets, and he had gotten here safely. Besides, if the kid could read at an adult level, he should be able to get back to the school by himself with no cars to contend with. Shouldn't he?

Aiden snuggled himself deeper into my arms. "Can't I stay here awhile longer with my mommy? Please?"

And then I had an inspired idea. Aiden could *help* me. "Aiden, I'll let you stay, but would you mind helping me with something?"

"Sure! What?"

I pulled another Police Beat binder out of the box. "Here. I'd like you to look for the name Yoke and or H. H. Holmes. Do you need me to write it down for you?"

"No, I can do it. Y-O-L-K. And—"

"No, Aiden, that's like egg yolk. This Yoke is Y-O-K-E."

"Okay, got it. And Holmes is H-O-L-M-E-S."

"Yes, exactly. Sit here beside me and go through it as fast as you can, but don't miss anything, okay?"

We sat there together, an hour went by quickly, and we had only each gone through one binder. I pulled out another one for each of us, and we started reading again.

After twenty minutes, Aiden looked up. "What if it has both names in it? Is that good?"

"What?" I took the binder out of his hands and read the passage he had indicated. *Floyd Yoke, part-time resident of Rutledge, tried and convicted of arson after setting fire to a park bench in Rutledge National Forest. The fire burned twenty-five hundred acres and destroyed two homes before it was contained. Floyd Yoke is the great grandson of the infamous H. H. Holmes who was a serial killer around the time of the 1893 Chicago World's Fair.*

I stopped reading and swallowed hard. This was it. This is what Ezra had been looking for. Floyd Yoke must be his grandfather, and it tied him back to the serial killer, Holmes.

"Is that it, Lorry—I mean Mommy? Is that what you were looking for?"

"This is *exactly* what I was looking for, Aiden! Great job! What a great kid you are!" I scooped him into my arms and hugged him. "Now, can you get back to school by yourself? Or would you like me to walk you back there?"

He shrugged. "I can get there by myself, because I always walk over here by myself. I'd like you to walk with me, but if you're busy, I'd understand."

After kissing him on the head, I gave him another hug and started to get up when I heard the bell announcing someone coming in the front door. Then I heard a voice call out "Hello? Anyone here?" It was the voice I recognized as Ezra Yoke, great great grandson of H. H. Holmes and the murderer of Betty and Gwen Wellesley.

CHAPTER FIFTY-FIVE

I LEANED OVER and whispered to Aiden, "Go back to the school as fast as you can and tell anyone you can to send the police here immediately! It's urgent! Can you do that?"

He stood up, but didn't understand, so I whispered, "*Now*, Aiden. It's important. Your mommy is in danger. Now, go!" Then I stood up and called, "I'll be right there, Ezra." I hoped that my voice didn't sound stressed, but how could it not? I was stressed to the max and scared out of my high heels.

Ezra walked toward the back to meet me. He had a smile on his face until he saw my face, which was probably devoid of all blood. I tried to smile, but I knew it looked fake. "Hello, Ezra," I said as casually as I could manage. "How are you today?"

The smile didn't fade from his face completely, but he nodded his head. "Hello, Lorry. How nice to see you," he said sardonically. Then he looked in the direction from where I had come. He saw the binders lying open on the floor where I'd left them. He put his arm around me and said, "I'd like to show you something upstairs."

Ezra led me toward the stairs.

He knew. I knew he knew, and he knew that I knew. And I was afraid if I went upstairs with him that I would end up at the *bottom* of the stairs in the same heap as Betty and Gwen. But there was nothing I could do about it. So I did what he asked and walked up the stairs in front of him. I only hoped that Aiden would get to school and tell someone, and that Sheriff Billy would get here in time. Except now that I thought about it, I didn't remember hearing the door close behind Aiden. Although I was probably just intent on the horror of seeing Ezra walk toward me. At least I hoped that's what it was. If Sheriff Billy didn't come to rescue me, I couldn't imagine who would.

Ezra leaned on the empty bookshelf and blocked my path to the stairs. There was nowhere for me to run to, even if I could run. Heels were not the best option if you wanted to run away from a killer. "So you found out, huh." The way he said it, it was not a question.

"I don't understand what difference it makes. It was a long time ago. It was more than a hundred years ago!" I had seen plenty of movies and read plenty of books on serial killers, and I thought if I could keep him talking I might have a chance.

"It's important to *me*," he said, his eyes narrowed. "I have a reason, and I want no one to find out about it. And if you are gone, and I find the excerpt, then I don't have to worry about it anymore. That's all." The smile on his face was frightening.

"You might as well tell me the reason, Ezra. Apparently, I won't be around to tell anyone."

He looked at his watch. "All right. We should have a minute, and it won't take longer than that."

I wasn't sure what he meant. What would take a minute? Telling me his story or killing me? I had to keep him talking so I wouldn't have to find out. "Go on."

He shrugged. "A woman contacted me and claimed to be my daughter. Now, I'm not an idiot, so I asked for a DNA test. The results aren't in yet. Even so, I have a feeling that she is. You know, I feel it here." He looked at me and put his hand on his heart.

A serial killer with heart. Great. Just what I needed. "I won't tell anyone about the excerpt. I promise. You can take it and go away, and no one will be the wiser."

He shook his head. "Sorry, Lorry, it's not as easy as that. Now, I just need one little tool—" He stepped in front of me toward the bookshelf, probably to get another rock. Being killed by a rock sounded a lot worse than being killed by a crystal. Facing the bookshelf, he reached in to retrieve the *crystal*, and suddenly there was a flurry of fur and claws and a shriek from Ezra.

Rocky, the flying kitty cat, came flying off the shelf he had been resting on, and with claws in attack mode, went straight for Ezra's face. Have I mentioned how much I love cats? Ezra scraped at his face to get the cat off and fell backwards as I heard footsteps running up the stairs. Little footsteps.

Ezra hit his head on the bookshelf behind him and lay on the floor, out cold. Rocky did a downward dog (would it be downward cat if a cat does it?) between me and Ezra. And the *little* footsteps on the stairs? Aiden came up holding a mop as a weapon. He must have been hiding out in the curtained closet by the back door. He took a couple of steps closer and kicked Ezra hard in the shin.

I wanted to tell him that it wasn't nice to kick someone

when they were down, but since Ezra had just tried to kill me, I couldn't get the words out. Instead, I picked Aiden up with one hand—he was still holding the mop— and Rocky with the other, and was planting kisses on both of them when I heard *big* footsteps on the stairs. It was Sheriff Billy.

When he saw me standing there, holding Aiden and Rocky, and Ezra on the floor just coming to, all he could do was laugh. That is, he laughed as he knelt down and put handcuffs on Ezra. When Billy looked at Ezra's face, with blood seeping out of the claw marks, he said, "I guess you three handled it. You didn't need me at all." He ruffled Aiden's hair, gave Rocky a quick pet, and looked at me seriously. "I'm glad you're okay, Lorry. It might not have turned out so favorably." Then he dragged Ezra to his feet and led him down the stairs.

I kissed Aiden and Rocky one more time and then sneezed again.

CHAPTER FIFTY-SIX

I SETTLED IN at my desk, still shaking. Billy had dropped Aiden off at school and taken Ezra in to process him. Over and over in my head, I went over how close I had come to *actual* death. The cat that I had disdained for so long had saved me. I would never hate cats again. I never realized they could be so awesome. After sneezing multiple times, I tried taking long, deep breaths. The same long, deep breaths that I had been trying to take for the past hour. Nothing could calm me down. Investigating murders had a lot more pitfalls than I had expected.

Someone coming through the door interrupted my thoughts. My cousin Kasey. As soon as I saw her, tears flowed from my eyes, and she wrapped her arms around me. "Lorry, I heard. It's all right, Lorry. You're all right. You're safe now." She spoke softly and petted my hair as she spoke, as I continued to cry on her shoulder. "You were so brave standing up to him. How did you capture him like that?"

I shook my head. "*I* didn't capture him. Rocky the cat clawed his face to shreds just as Ezra was about to kill me. I owe everything to that cat."

"Aren't you allergic to cats?"

I nodded and sneezed and then shook my head again after rubbing my itching eyes. "Not anymore. I will not let it get to me anymore. I owe that cat my life!" As I sneezed again, I pulled away from Kasey. I didn't want to get her bright yellow waitress uniform all sneezy.

"Well, I'm glad you're safe—and *alive*! This was just a quick break, though. I have to run."

Glancing out the window, I saw the red mustang there —the one I'd seen Eddie driving before. "Hey, Kasey? Is Eddie in there?"

She shook her head. "No, why?"

"Because that red mustang is out there, and I've seen him driving it a couple of times."

"Oh! It belongs to—" She stopped suddenly and looked at me guiltily.

"Go on, Kasey. I've filed for divorce. I'm through with him. I saw him driving away with a blond. Now tell me."

"It belongs to Rita Croft—Eddie's new girlfriend."

I nodded. "Renee Croft's sister."

"Yes, that's right. Lorry, I have to go. Glad you're safe! Bye!" And she slid out the door.

The afternoon progressed and the shaking finally stopped. I thought about Rita Croft and Eddie. It made me happy that she was with him—not that I cared about the jerk's happiness, but because maybe he would eventually leave me alone if he had someone else. But Rita's family was very wealthy. Why would he need *my* money? Probably because he didn't want her supporting him, although it never bothered him that *I* supported him. What a fool I was!

Was? Who was I kidding? Didn't I just fall for a suave,

sophisticated guy who tried to kill me? I thought I should probably stay away from men for a while until I got my head straight. Apparently, I still couldn't trust myself where men were concerned. But I would never go back to Eddie; that much I knew. So I had taken a step forward. Well, maybe half a step.

A courier truck had double parked outside, and a courier rushed into the building. It was the same guy. Before he even asked, I dug in my purse for my driver's license and handed it to him. He smiled and said thank you without even looking at it. Then he handed me the envelope. It was from my mother's attorneys again.

Before the guy was even back in his truck, I had the outer envelope *and* the inner envelope opened. I pulled out the letter. *Dear Ms. Lockharte, It has come to our attention that you are in the process of adopting a child. All of your expenses from here forward will be paid. And since it would be inappropriate for you to remain at your present domicile, the funds will be made available for you to purchase your own home. We understand that you have turned Mr. Edward Keeley away when he approached you for money. That is as it should be. If we ever find that you have re-established friendly relations with said Edward Keeley, all expenses and funding will be terminated. Sincerely—*

Tears streamed down my face anew. I couldn't believe all this was happening. A couple of weeks ago I was destitute and mourning the loss of my marriage. It was a bad marriage, but it was mine. And as much of a jerk as Eddie was, I had been afraid to leave—afraid to be on my own. And when the break came, and I found that he had taken all the money out of the bank and hadn't paid the mortgage, I thought it was the worst thing in the world. I had even considered suicide. And now—now my life couldn't be better. Not only would I have my own home again, but I would have a wonderful little boy to share it with. The tears streamed down my face.

Rocky the cat appeared out of nowhere and jumped up on my lap. I kissed him on the top of his head and stroked his silky fur. Yes, it was silky. He arched his back under my hand and purred. Is there anything in this world better than a purring cat? I never knew it could be so comforting. Then I sneezed.

Petra walked in the door with her face exuberant. "Lorry! I heard you caught the killer, and it was that creep that Betty had the argument with! Good job! Tell me!" Then she blinked and looked at me again. "What are you doing holding Rocky? I thought you were allergic."

I sneezed, and then I told her how Rocky had saved the day, and how Aiden had kicked the killer in the shin. "What I don't understand, though, is why Billy showed up."

"Oh! *I* know that part! Michael Wellesley showed you some kind of paper he found?"

I nodded. "Yeah. It was a message for murder. That information was what got Betty and Gwen killed."

"Well, after he showed it to you, he took it to Billy. But Billy wasn't available to read it until later. When he did, he rushed right over."

"Oh, okay. I wondered how that happened."

Petra smiled at me. "I'm glad you're okay, Lorry. Oh! There was something else. Some woman had claimed to be his daughter or something? Anyway, the DNA test came back negative!"

So he killed the two sisters for nothing. Nobody would have cared or been looking for his relationship to the serial killer. What irony. In his effort to separate himself from his murderous relative, he became just like him. Ah well. There was nothing I could do about it now.

"Look at what I just received," I said as I handed her the letter.

She smiled and gave me a high-five. "Happy. From the fourteenth century. Originally meaning lucky, favored by fortune, prosperous. It fits! That's so awesome, Lorry! What could possibly be better? Wow! Congratulations!" She started to go to her office and then turned back. "Oh, by the way. There's a woman out there looking for you, but I didn't know if she was tied up with your ex, so I didn't say anything." Petra pointed out the window.

Leaning forward in my chair, I looked out the window. Even if I hadn't seen the dog, I would have recognized the woman. Without saying another word, I jumped up and ran out the door.

The woman saw me coming. "Lorry! I was hoping I could find you."

But she was talking to the back of my head, because I was down on my knees holding and petting the dog while he licked me all over the face. All I could say was "Bingo. Bingo. Bingo."

"Lorry, as I was saying, my family is moving to the South, and we can't take him with us. Would you want him or could you find a good home for him? I didn't want to leave him at the shelter."

"Thank you, thank you, thank you," I said while still stroking and kissing Bingo. "Yes, yes, I will take him." I glanced up briefly and through my tears, I choked out, "I never got over him or got over that Eddie made me give him away. I never got over it." I shook my head, and kept crying as I petted the dog that was my Soul Dog. "Thank you for bringing him back to me."

"I've got to run now, Lorry. Glad you got him back. He's been a great dog." And the woman—I couldn't remember her name—walked away.

My life was now complete. Favored by fortune, indeed. It had gotten even better than five minutes before when Petra asked how it could possibly get any better. It had. Wow. It had.

If you liked this book and feel so inclined, please leave a review on Amazon. Thank you! I appreciate it!

And if you'd like to know when the next Rutledge Historical Society mystery comes out, sign up for the mailing list: http://www.ralstonstorepublishing.com/mysteryL.html

Read the second and third Rutledge Historical Society mysteries:

Death over Divorce
When a dead man that she knows falls out of Lorry Lockharte's new car right in front of the sheriff, it doesn't look good. Still, being hauled into the sheriff's station isn't what Lorry had expected. After a lawyer comes out of nowhere to get her released, Lorry struggles to prove her innocence and find the real killer.

Kousins Kan't Kill
When Lorry Lockharte's cousin, Kasey, is accused of murder, Lorry feels like once again she must work to find the murderer. Did Kasey do it, or is she truly innocent as she claims? Lorry isn't so sure about this one. Not only did Kasey have the opportunity and the motive, but she picked up the murder weapon. Will Lorry find the murderer only to discover that it really is Kasey?

Other books published by Ralston Store Publishing:

Time Travel Sweet Romance
Cowgirls in Time Series by Erica Einhorn
A Chill Wind
Wind Beneath My Wings
Against the Wind
The Healing Wind
Ride Like the Wind
Wind of Change
The Way the Wind Blows

Caregiving
The Journey that Matters by Jodie Lightener

Suspense
Darkness in the Light by J.K. Lincoln

India
Not My Guru by Parvati Hill

Women's Fiction/Reincarnation
Two Lifetimes, One Love by Thea Thaxton

Yoga Books
Bathroom Yoga
Airplane Yoga
Wheelchair Yoga
Essential Yoga on Horseback
Exercises for Therapeutic Riding

Recipe for Noodle Knoodle

One pound hamburger
One can sliced ripe olives
One can tomato sauce
One package noodles
One can corn
A little marjoram and thyme wouldn't hurt!

Brown hamburger and cook noodles. Mix together browned hamburger, cooked noodles, sliced olives, corn, and tomato sauce. Put into a greased casserole dish. Cook at 350 degrees for thirty minutes.

www.ingramcontent.com/pod-product-compliance
Lightning Source LLC
Chambersburg PA
CBHW070800200626
46811CB00023B/311